Endless NIGHTMARE

REVISED EDITION (2020)

PATRICIA L. POWELL

ENDLESS NIGHTMARE
REVISED EDITION (2020)

iUniverse books may be ordered through booksellers or by contacting:

iUniverse
1663 Liberty Drive
Bloomington, IN 47403
www.iuniverse.com
844-349-9409

ISBN: 978-1-6632-0525-4 (sc)
ISBN: 978-1-6632-0526-1 (hc)
ISBN: 978-1-6632-0527-8 (e)

Library of Congress Control Number: 2020913385

Print information available on the last page.

iUniverse rev. date: 07/28/2020

PROLOGUE

Looking out her bedroom window, May Willard readied herself to go jogging despite the cold, cloudy day urging her to stay indoors. As she finished tying her shoes, the less-than-welcoming weather invited her outside for an early morning jog in her late husband's memory. Glancing at the closet where he had kept his jogging suit, May was reminded of the many times he would push her to join him, only for her to return his endless pleadings with whining about needing her beauty sleep.

Oh, how she now wished she would've said yes every time, taking in the crisp air as they enjoyed simply being together. May found herself with a deep ache in her heart as she thought about George and those missed moments. She could just imagine the two of them getting back from their jog and their maid, Ms. Cecilia, having their breakfast of poached eggs and orange juice ready for them, with an accompanying pot of tea and a plate of toast.

Ever since his death a few years ago, life had become dull and monotonous for May. Prior to George passing away from sudden heart failure at the age of fifty-six, the two had talked about traveling to France to visit her Parisian cousin. Sadly, that trip now felt like a passing cloud, as the excitement for traveling anywhere was reduced to a momentary sigh.

Heading downstairs, now ready to face the outside world, May looked through the parlor and could see Ms. Cecilia in the kitchen eating her breakfast. "Ms. Cecilia, I'm going to go for a jog. I'll probably be back around nine."

"Madam May, would you like me to have your breakfast ready for you when you return?" She stopped eating. "If so, I will have to go to the store."

"That's quite all right. There's a French café George and I passed whenever we took our strolls. I'll probably just pop in for a quick pastry and a cappuccino. Would you like anything?"

"No thank you, madam."

Accepting her answer, May opened the door as if she were about to embark on a journey and then disappeared from her maid's sight. Taking a deep breath, she imagined seeing the world through George's eyes and thought about what he might've noticed as he observed the world around him. As she began her jog, she realized that having company might provide more enjoyment. Stopping by a friend's house, she rang the doorbell. Checking her watch to see that it was only 8:15, May realized that it would be a long jog if her dear friend couldn't accompany her.

Watching the door open, she saw her friend's daughter appear on the other side.

"Hi, Carla, is your mom home? I thought I would go for a jog and was wondering if she would like to join me."

"Sorry, but my mom's not feeling well. Maybe another time, though."

"Another time it is, and I hope she feels better."

With a smile, Carla replied. "Thanks. I'll let her know you stopped by. See you later, Mrs. Willard."

Returning the pleasantry, May said goodbye before jogging off. As she ran the path George would've taken, her heart felt as if she was saying goodbye to him all over again. Then, as if the weather knew what her heart was going through, she began to feel droplets of water hit her skin and her windbreaker. Shrugging it off, she kept running. But as she reached a bridge, the water droplets became more numerous. Realizing that the rain wasn't going to let up anytime soon, she decided to use her windbreaker as cover and headed for the café.

Imagining the warmth of the café as her French breakfast allowed her time to dry, she could just picture her and George laughing, the two feeling like kids again.

With a tear for the thought and sadness in her heart for missing him so dearly, May suddenly felt someone grab her from behind. Screaming, she immediately let go of the windbreaker and did her best to break free. Feeling hands find their way around her neck, she did what she could to call for help. But with the windbreaker making it difficult for her to see, she found her ability to fight for her life futile.

As it became harder and harder for her to breathe, May realized that she had no choice but to let go. With her screaming for help now turning into a whisper, she felt her life begin to leave her. The whispers now gasps, May tried to gulp down one last breath before succumbing to the pressure against her throat.

With her body now lifeless and the windbreaker on the ground beside her, her killer put her windbreaker back on her before throwing her over the bridge to watch the river claim her. Taking a brief moment to make sure there were no witnesses, the killer hurried away.

CHAPTER 1

Deciding to make a quick grocery run, as the cupboards bordered on empty, Ms. Cecilia jotted down a few items in hopes that she could get back to the house before May returned. Knowing that May would take her time once she had her pastry in one hand and a hot cappuccino waiting on a saucer for her consumption, Ms. Cecilia made quick work of checking off her grocery list.

With a smile at the thought of her enjoying her morning treats at the Parisian café in honor of George, Ms. Cecilia returned to the house and began filling the cupboards with the groceries. But as time passed and she had yet to hear the sound of the front door opening and closing, she began to worry.

For a moment, she wondered if something might've happened to her. Just as quickly discarding that possibility, she decided to clean the house. But as the fleeting thought turned into a list of chores that still needed to be done, she heard the doorbell ring.

Thinking it strange that May would ring her own doorbell, Ms. Cecilia took a break from her housekeeping to see who it was.

"Hi, I'm Detective John Murray. Are you the owner of this residence?"

"No, I'm just the maid. Why, is there a problem?"

"I'm afraid so. A woman named May Willard was found floating in the river at Culver Park around eight thirty this morning. Her driver's license gave this address as her residence."

"Oh no! Madam May! No!" Ms. Cecilia immediately fell to her knees.

"I'm sorry for your loss." He was clearly unsure how to comfort her. "Uh, at your convenience, I'll need you to come down to the station to identify her body."

"Yes, sir."

"As well as answer some questions." He sighed as he watched her remain distraught.

She nodded, tears saturating her face. "I understand. If you'd like, I can answer them now."

Nodding, Detective Murray followed her inside. "I'll need your name and how long you've been Ms. Willard's maid."

"Cecilia Ann Riley ... and for seventeen years. Our families knew each other. When my parents fell on hard times because my mom had to quit her job to care for my younger sister Francine, who became stricken with cancer, May was gracious enough to let me come work for her."

Nodding, he wrote it down.

"May I ask how she was found?" Ms. Cecilia felt dreadful just having to ask the question.

"A homeless man looking for shelter from the rain saw Ms. Willard's body floating in the river. We were fortunate that her body hadn't been in it that long." He grimaced, wondering if that was too much information to give her.

Nodding, Ms. Cecilia dabbed her eyes.

"My next question may upset you, but I need to know ..."

"Go on." She figured she knew what he was about to ask.

"Where were you around eight thirty this morning?"

"Prior to May going for her walk, I was here, and then I went grocery shopping before returning."

"I'll need the name of the grocery store you went to."

"Yes, sir."

Providing him the grocery store's name, she did her best to remember the times she had arrived and left. Fortunately, the detective was able to reassure her that he would be able to check the grocery store's surveillance cameras for more accurate information.

"Finally, does Ms. Willard have any family I can contact for arrangements to be made?"

"Yes, she has three nieces who live in New York City. Mind you, they haven't seen her in several years, but they are still family. Oh, and she has a cousin in Paris, France. She and her late husband, George, talked about visiting her before his death a few years ago."

"Thank you." He scribbled the information down. "Would you happen to have their names and contact information?"

"Oh, yes. I'm sorry. Sarah, Melissa, and Jessica. Sarah is the oldest. She's twenty-eight, and Melissa and Jessica are twins; they're twenty-six. As for their contact information, I'll have to look for that. Madam May kept that information in her office."

"Well, as soon as you find it, just let me know. Her nieces will need to be contacted ASAP." Taking a business card from a coat pocket to give to her, he began to get up.

"Actually ..." Her tears were keeping her eyes moistened.

He stopped in his tracks.

"Would you mind if I contacted them myself? After all, I wouldn't be a complete stranger to them."

"Uh, yeah. Sure, that'd be fine." He quickly nodded. "Here's my business card in case you end up needing it."

Nodding in return, she took the card. The white business card with its black print and standard design represented the detective's personality well.

"Detective Murray?"

"Yes?"

"Do you know if she was ... murdered?"

"Unofficially, Ms. Riley, it does look to be that way, but I can't give you a definitive answer until an autopsy is completed. I'm sorry."

"I understand. I just wanted to know. Madam May left this house in good enough spirits for a widow, so I don't believe suicide was ever a consideration for her."

"Thank you. I'll keep that in mind." He headed for the door. "Once again, I'm sorry for your loss."

Nodding again, Ms. Cecilia watched the detective leave before closing the door.

Realizing that May's office was locked and only May had the key, Ms. Cecilia took a bobby pin from her hair and wrestled with the lock until it opened.

Turning the knob, she opened the door to an organized room. Immediately, she could see the accolades that adorned the walls. From her master's degree in social work to the pictures she had of her family and friends, May Christine Willard had lived a prosperous life.

"Hopefully, she'll make this easy on me." She began searching for the sisters' contact information.

Now that May Willard was dead, she needed to find out why May needed to keep her out of her office. May Willard had secrets, and she was going to find out what they were.

CHAPTER 2

Looking down at the names and contact information for May's nieces in May's planner, Ms. Cecilia contemplated whom to call first.

The eldest, Sarah Parker, was an established human rights lawyer at Benson and Parker. Upon completing law school, her aunt had connected her with a highly prominent law firm in the city, allowing Sarah the ability to build her résumé until she eventually became the law firm's first female partner. She always credited her passion and love for advocating for the less fortunate as a direct result of watching the way her aunt had lived her life.

"But would she even have the time to take my call?" she wondered aloud. "I'm sure she'd be quite busy and I'd probably have to leave a message with her assistant."

Glancing next at Melissa's name and number, Ms. Cecilia wondered if she'd be the easier sister to contact. She remembered her as a curious little girl. Whenever May made a trip the city's library, Melissa would always beg to go with her. She loved reading anything she could get her hands on. From fairy tales as a little girl to teen romance novels once she became of age, Melissa always had a book in her hands.

It was especially heartwarming to watch May sit and read a book with her as a child, encouraging her love for reading and learning about new things and exciting adventures. A few years ago, Melissa had taken her love for books and translated it into owning her own children's bookstore.

"Or I could call Jessica ..."

Jessica had taken a different path entirely. Instead of committing herself to a few arduous years of postsecondary school or following a childhood passion, she had eventually found herself taking an art class at a local college.

However, without the drive to follow a passion, Jessica had embraced being a free spirit like her aunt. Instead of maintaining a long-term job that could eventually turn into a career, she had instead opted for short-term gigs that gave her the opportunity to experience more of the city and continuously meet new people.

"But would she be able to answer her phone while in class?"

Ms. Cecilia thought about it for a brief second more before deciding to call Melissa first. It had been a long time since she'd last spoken to her.

Using the office phone, Ms. Cecilia called Melissa. She wondered if Melissa would even remember her voice but then realized it was a silly thought given that she had known Melissa from when she was a mere baby.

After only two rings, she heard a phone being picked up and a voice greeting her. "Hello, this is Melissa at Parker's Children's Bookstore. How may I help you?"

"Ms. Melissa, it's Ms. Cecilia."

"Ms. Cecilia! It's been a long time."

"Yes, I know. It's been years, and unfortunately, I have some very sad news to share with you."

"Did something happen to Aunt May?" Melissa knew of no other reason for her aunt's maid to call her.

"Yes, Ms. Melissa. I'm sorry to say that something did happen to her." She took a breath. "Your aunt May was found dead this morning while on a jog through the park."

"Dead? Are you sure?"

"Yes. Unfortunately, I am." Her tears returned at just having to repeat the words.

Shock and disbelief immediately hit her system. Her aunt May had played such a pivotal role in her life. Without her guidance, she would've never become the owner of her own bookstore.

"How?" Tears began running down her skin.

"The detective who informed me of her passing told me a homeless man found her. He said, unofficially, that he thinks she was murdered."

She purposefully kept the details to herself because she didn't think Melissa could handle hearing the rest of what Detective Murray had told her until she had time to let it sink in.

As Ms. Cecilia waited for her response, she could hear Melissa crying in the background.

"I am so sorry, Ms. Melissa. I know it's such dreadful news to hear."

Sniffling, Melissa said, "Thank you for letting me know. It makes me wish my sisters and I had taken the time to visit her over the past few years."

"I know, and your aunt May understood."

"Thank you, Ms. Cecilia, for trying to make this a little easier for me."

"Of course, Ms. Melissa."

Hanging up after telling Ms. Cecilia goodbye, Melissa still couldn't believe that her own aunt had been murdered. Collapsing to the floor, she buried her face in her hands. With tears keeping her vision blurry, the memories of her visits to her aunt and uncle's house flashed through her mind.

And now I'm going to have to tell Jessica and Sarah. Just the thought brought on more tears.

Melissa could only imagine their reactions the moment she gave them the horrible news. Their aunt May had been the driving force behind their close-knit bond. She had been a pillar of strength for each sister as the girls individually found their place in the world.

But as her grief ensued, Melissa realized that she had forgotten to find out how her aunt had been murdered. *Does she even know? And if she does, why didn't she tell me?*

Either way, she couldn't believe that her aunt was actually gone and that her and her sisters' last visit to their aunt and uncle's house had been the last time they would get to visit her.

Getting up off the floor, Melissa wiped the rest of her tears from her face and looked around her small bookstore. It had a quaint charm her aunt would've loved, but most of all, she could imagine the pride that would've shown so brightly on her face.

"I just wish she could've seen it for herself!" With her hands on her hips, Melissa took a deep breath and decided to close early. It was one of the things she loved about being the owner.

Making the brief walk to her car, Melissa turned back around to take in the brick building that had eventually come to house her bookstore. She had remembered seeing it first as an open space to lease. With two huge windows in the storefront and a wooden door to welcome customers inside, it was the perfect look for her to share her passion with those who loved reading as much as she did.

With a sigh for what she wished could've been, Melissa continued and got in her car. Taking a moment before turning on the engine, she prepared herself for the drive home.

She and her sisters hadn't had any contact with their aunt since their mom and dad had divorced, causing their mom to have a nervous breakdown that put her in a psychiatric facility in Maine. Meanwhile, their dad eventually remarried and moved to Florida with his new wife. Their once close-knit family was now states apart, as Melissa and her sisters had found their lives in New York City.

As Melissa drove home, she cried at the thought of having to tell Jessica and Sarah about their aunt May's death. Just imagining what might have happened to her, she had absolutely no idea how she was going to break the news to them without becoming a complete mess herself.

With a fifteen-minute drive to figure it out, Melissa thought back to the days when Aunt May had been a key figure in their lives and how she would've handled telling them this kind of news herself.

As Melissa reworked the wording in her head, back in California the medical examiner officially resolved May Willard's cause of death the second her neck became visible. Whoever had killed her had pressed so hard against her neck that her skin easily showed signs of agitation with its red marks and bruising.

Taking off May's running shoes, the medical examiner removed her jumpsuit. As her pale skin took in the morgue's artificial lighting, her graying hair spoke of her weathered life at fifty-four, while her five-foot, seven-inch frame and hazel eyes completed her basic stats. Adding her undergarments to the rest of her clothes, the medical examiner completed a thorough autopsy of how her body was physically affected during her last minutes of life and then secured them in a large Ziploc bag.

With each note jotted down for what was visible, the medical examiner spoke into a recorder about every step taken and every detail noticed. Once May's outer condition was documented, a toxicology report was ordered.

When the examination reached its end, the medical examiner prepared her body for a morgue drawer.

CHAPTER 3

Finding a place to park in front of a grayish-white stucco building, Melissa locked her car before heading up to her and her sisters' fourth-floor apartment. They had been fortunate to have their aunt May's connections, allowing them the comfort of a three-bedroom, one-bathroom apartment on the Lower East Side. Though their view consisted of trees and another apartment building, their apartment's ample square footage left them with no reason to complain.

Taking her time going up the stairs, Melissa braced herself for the disheartening news she was about to share. With each step, she pictured the reactions the sisters would give once she told them about their aunt May. Sarah would immediately take on the role of the mother hen, whereas Jessica would probably show some disbelief and defiance for their parents' own destructive behavior as the cause.

"I'm home." Melissa unlocked the door to find Jessica on the couch watching TV and Sarah making dinner.

"How's the world of selling children's books?" Jessica asked. Her gaze remained focused on a TV show she had found herself immersed in.

"It's fine. It's a continuous struggle to remain relevant, but overall, I love it."

With the news on the forefront of her mind, she knew her emotions would eventually signal to her sisters that something was wrong.

Thinking about Melissa's contentment in her life, Jessica was left with little to wonder as to whether Melissa had found her purpose in life.

"Melissa, I'm making mom's chicken and dumplings for dinner, so I hope you're hungry," Sarah called out from the kitchen.

"Sounds yummy ... but guys, I've got some bad news." She took a deep breath.

"What's wrong?" Sarah immediately came out of the kitchen.

Jessica just as quickly turned her attention from the TV to Melissa.

Rehashing what Ms. Cecilia had told her, Melissa felt a new onslaught of tears making their appearance on her face.

"When did she call you?" Sarah asked.

"About thirty minutes ago." She remembered breaking down behind the counter.

"Did she tell you how?" Jessica asked. She didn't want to imagine that there could be anyone cruel enough to purposely take their aunt's life.

"No ... and I didn't think to ask."

"That's probably for the better," Jessica pointed out.

"Maybe." Melissa sat down on the couch next to Jessica.

Putting her head on Jessica's shoulder, Melissa let the tears flow as Jessica did her best to comfort her.

"It probably is, Melissa, but we'll likely find that out once we get to California," Sarah concluded.

"Right now I don't know if I even want to know how she was murdered. It's already too much that she's gone!" Jessica ran to her room and slammed the door. Her own memories made her not want to deal with the past.

"California. It's been years since we've been to her and Uncle George's house." Sarah took over comforting Melissa. Just the state's name reminded her of memories she had of visiting their aunt and uncle. "When is Ms. Cecilia expecting us out there?"

"I would imagine as soon as possible," she answered.

With both her aunt and uncle now gone, Jessica cried into her pillow. She had been close with their aunt May, with each sharing a rebellious nature that allowed their wild and free-spirited side to be expressed. Aunt May was the only family member who truly understood her. With her now gone, Jessica couldn't help but feel all alone.

"I'll go talk to her," Melissa decided, leaving Sarah to use their dinner's preparation as a coping mechanism.

As the oldest of the three, Sarah felt accountable for her younger sisters. That had been especially reiterated to her whenever they visited their aunt May and she instilled in her the importance of familial responsibility as the eldest Parker sister.

"Jessica?" Melissa softly knocked on her bedroom door.

"What?" She did her best to clear her tears away.

"Are you okay? I know Aunt May's death is a shock to each of us." Melissa slowly opened her door. Closing it, she took a seat on her bed.

"Okay as I can be, I guess."

Jessica saw her ruined mascara when she looked down at her hand and saw the black smearing.

"I think going back to her house will be good for us. You know, cathartic. After all, we did have some fun times there." Melissa smiled, hoping to cheer her up.

"Yeah, I remember that water fight we all got into as kids. Aunt May joined right in as Uncle George and our parents just laughed."

"Jessica, you and her were so much alike. I was actually kind of envious of your relationship."

"You were? As the older twin, I always felt as if I didn't have my own voice. I felt like Mom and Dad had certain expectations for me ... expectations that I could never meet. Aunt May understood that."

"Wow, and here I thought I was the one who was lost."

"You ... lost? Melissa, you own your own bookstore, for crying out loud! How could you possibly be lost?"

"I meant back then, Jessica. I had no clue what my path was. I saw Sarah barreling toward her passion and you just having fun living life. Me, I was just there, observing everyone around me, trying to figure out who I was supposed to be."

"Wow, Melissa, I honestly had no idea."

Jessica's tears were now gone, as her mascara had dried to her face.

"It's fine. I obviously eventually figured out my path. And now it's your turn."

"Who says I haven't figured out my path yet?"

"Jessica, you have never held down a full-time job for more than six months."

"So? I like keeping my options open."

"But there's no stability in that." Melissa thought about Jessica's long list of employers. Despite her being an art student at a school on the Upper East Side, Jessica was still trying to find her place within that community.

Smiling, Jessica gave Melissa a hug. "We'd better start packing since I'm sure Sarah's already looked up flights and booked the first one available."

Laughing, Melissa said, "I wouldn't doubt it." She left Jessica's room.

With a feeling of homecoming, Jessica grabbed a suitcase from her closet and began packing for their trip to California. Though it had been so long since she'd last visited her aunt and uncle's house, she could just picture her aunt May with open arms, welcoming them home.

CHAPTER 4

"How are we going to find them in this airport?" Detective Murray's twenty-seven-year-old nephew, Nick Powell, asked as they entered San Francisco International Airport.

After Ms. Cecilia had informed Melissa of her aunt's passing, she had used the card Detective Murray had given her for his assistance in picking them up at the airport. Just moments before calling Melissa, she had found out that her ailing mother needed her to pick up her medication for her. She would have to wait until they arrived at the house to reunite with them.

"With this." He gave his nephew a sign that read PARKER SISTERS. "Hold that up once we get to baggage claim."

Nodding, Nick followed his uncle through the busy airport until they reached others waiting for arriving passengers. Holding up the sign, he curiously watched for three girls who might be telltale sisters. But as the waiting lengthened, he wondered if they had missed their flight or decided not to come after all. "Are you sure they're coming? Maybe they changed their minds or gave you the wrong flight information."

"Keep holding up that sign, Nick. When Ms. Willard's maid called me with their flight information, she made sure to confirm it prior to hanging up."

"And she didn't give you any descriptions while she was on the phone with you?"

"Nope. I don't really think her mindset was on that."

"Oh, right. Never mind, then." Nick remembered the reason for the girls' last-minute flight.

Wishing he had thought to ask for a description of each, all Detective Murray could do was work on his patience. Fortunately for him and his nephew, they soon saw three girls making their way in their direction.

"Two of them are identical twins." Nick pointed out as he watched the three girls stay together despite becoming meshed into the crowd of people anxious to retrieve their luggage.

"Apparently." Detective Murray sighed. *Why didn't Ms. Willard's maid tell me that they were identical twins from the get-go?*

Seeing the sign with their last name on it, Sarah directed her sisters to it. "Are you Detective Murray?" she asked him while Nick continued holding the sign.

He wore his usual suit and tie, showing off his older age, whereas Nick had dressed in a more casual outfit of a maroon polo shirt and jeans.

"Yes, and this is my nephew, Nicholas Powell. He goes by Nick." Detective Murray shook her hand.

"I'm Sarah and these are my sisters, Melissa and Jessica."

Melissa and Jessica followed suit.

"I'm sorry for the unexpected trip, and that your aunt's maid couldn't be here to greet you instead. She had some last-minute family business to take care of herself."

"Thank you, and Ms. Cecilia told us." Sarah nodded her understanding, waving off his condolences. "Our aunt would just want us to make the most of it. Besides, it's been since we were teens that we've been back here, so the reunion's been a long time coming."

"I understand." Detective Murray headed over to their assigned carousel to claim their luggage. Leaving Jessica to meet Nick, Sarah and Melissa joined him.

When Jessica's attention shifted to Nick, it was as if a shot of electricity had hit her body. It was an understatement to say that he was cute. As she slid her hand into his to greet him, their eyes locked.

It was as if the artificial light streaming through the terminal shown on him like a spotlight. The light enhanced his short, wavy chestnut hair and made his brown eyes stand out. Meeting him was unlike anything she'd ever experienced before.

"Jessica." She smiled.

She could already feel her heart beating faster and her pulse racing as she took in the feel of his skin against hers and the way his eyes kept their connection.

Smiling, she forgot about joining her sisters and the detective to get her suitcases. She was too entranced by Nick's presence.

Looking back into Nick's brown eyes, Jessica found herself entranced by them. They held a mischievous glimmer that instantly attracted her.

"Nick." He found he couldn't look away.

Jessica's eyes had drawn him in, and they weren't letting him go.

Melissa interrupted their moment. "Jessica, the detective and Sarah have our luggage."

"Oh, he does? Okay." She shyly turned away from Nick and took her suitcase. Their hands slowly released as she left his presence.

"Looks like someone's got the hots for the detective's nephew," Melissa teased her as they all followed Detective Murray and his nephew out of the airport.

Jessica couldn't help but give her a big smile in return. "He is kind of cute."

"Kind of? The two of you looked oblivious to the world around you back there." She smirked.

Not wanting any of the others to overhear their conversation, Jessica whispered her response. "Okay, so I think he's really hot. His brown eyes just grabbed mine." She practically giggled it out.

"Maybe he can be your silver lining to this trip?" She shrugged.

"Maybe." Jessica smiled.

CHAPTER 5

Sitting in the back seat of Detective Murray's car with her sisters, the drive to the two-story light maroon Victorian house was filled with restlessness and curiosity for Jessica—restlessness because she couldn't help but revert her eyes back to Nick's profile as she sat behind the driver's seat and curiosity for how the timeworn house now looked.

Part of her wished either Melissa or Sarah had sat up front so Nick could sit next to her, while the other part realized how nerve-racking that probably would've been. Just taking in his chestnut hair made her realize that had he sat next to her, it would've been excessively inviting to her fingers.

Detective Murray interrupted Jessica's thoughts. "Your aunt's maid will be meeting us at the house to let you in. If you need anything, you have my number, and Nick will be available as well. He'll make sure to give you his contact information before we leave."

"Thank you, Detective. We appreciate that," Sarah replied.

Melissa teasingly whispered to Jessica, "I know *you* do, and now you won't have to wonder if he'll ask you for yours."

"Shhh, you might make him look back here," she whispered back. Glancing at him, she wondered if he was fighting the urge to do just that.

"In that case, maybe I should whisper louder."

"Melissa, stop it."

"Okay, okay. I'll stop."

Resting her head on Jessica's shoulder, Melissa stayed quiet for the remainder of the drive.

Half an hour later, Detective Murray turned onto their aunt and uncle's street. Within minutes, he was pulling his car into the driveway alongside Ms. Cecilia's car and parking. As he turned off the engine, everyone got out.

The exterior of the house looked the same from when the sisters had last visited, even down to the extremely well-manicured landscaping. Their aunt May was meticulous about the way the front yard looked. Since it was the first thing a visitor would see, she made sure that there would be no faults with their first impression. It had to be immaculate.

"It still smells like her," Melissa pointed out as the aroma of May's favorite flowers reminded her of familiarity.

Looking at the floral art surrounding the front of the house May had prided herself on, Sarah could remember planting flowers with her as a child, watching her dig the holes and then spreading the seeds. It was a memory with her aunt that she was grateful to have.

Knocking on the door, Detective Murray waited for Ms. Cecilia to let them in. Hearing her acknowledge his presence, it wasn't long before she was opening the door and welcoming the group into the house.

The front entryway of the interior immediately welcomed guests with a redwood floor covered by a white and light blue Parisian rug. An oak staircase led the eye up to the second floor, and various floral paintings by French artists lined the walls.

"Your aunt sure loved her flowers!" Nick had clearly noticed the abundance of floral displays.

From the front yard to the home's decor, flowers were definitely not in short supply at the Willard household.

"Yes, May did love her flowers." Ms. Cecilia nodded, taking a breath as if she were breathing in each painting's aroma. "It is so good to see you girls. I've missed you three so very much!"

Taking a moment to hug each sister as the girls took in the familiarity of what they considered their second home, Ms. Cecilia felt tears at just the sight of them. "It is so good to have you three back here. I so wish it could've been to see your aunt, but just the same, I've missed you three terribly." The reunion released her emotions.

"It's nice to see you too, Ms. Cecilia," Melissa returned with a sweet smile. "I know you were such a huge part of our aunt's life."

"Ah, yes. Your aunt and I were such dear friends. It is so terrible what happened to her." Dabbing her eyes, she put a hand over one of Melissa's.

As Jessica watched Nick take in her aunt's chosen decor, she thought about nonchalantly brushing up against his side. She wondered if she could somehow slip her hand into his without anyone else noticing. Just the thought made her heart beat faster. She was definitely attracted to Nick Powell. However, just as she was about to slide up next to him, his uncle stopped her.

"Girls, Ms. Cecilia, I've got to get back to the station. Ms. Cecilia, were you intending on staying here while the girls are making arrangements for their aunt?"

"I hadn't actually thought about it. But I can probably arrange to stay with my sister in order to give them some time to give her a proper goodbye." Ms. Cecilia had been using one of the guest rooms during her employment under the Willards.

"I'm sure they would appreciate that as well." Detective Murray glanced in their direction. "Nick, why don't you go get their bags?"

Nodding, Nick headed back to the car. Popping the trunk, he took out their suitcases and carry-ons. *I wonder how long they're planning on staying.* The luggage felt as if it had been packed for more than just a week's time.

Jessica enjoyed watching him bring in their luggage. It meant that she got to see his biceps being put to work.

"I'll make sure to keep you all updated on any progress made." The detective handed Jessica his card before heading for the door.

"Thank you, Detective. We appreciate it."

Nodding, he said, "Of course."

"Um, what about Nick's contact information? Since we've only visited Aunt May when we've come to California, we won't know our way around the city," Melissa chimed in for Jessica's sake.

"Oh, right. Nick, once you're finished with their bags, do you mind giving one of them your cell number?"

"Not at all, Uncle John." His mind went to Jessica.

"Good. You take care of that and I'll wait for you in the car." Detective Murray closed the door behind him.

"Nick, why don't you give your number to Jessica?" Melissa suggested after watching him bring in the last bag. "Sarah and I need to check with Ms. Cecilia on what groceries are needed."

Shaking her head at her sister for her clear matchmaking motive, Jessica turned to Nick. "Hi again."

"Hey, so as my uncle said, if you or your sisters need anything, my number is ..." He waited for her to get out her phone so she could program it in.

He had thought about asking her for her number, but thanks to Melissa, he didn't have to now.

"Thanks." She wondered how much alone time they would have.

"Though why did your uncle enlist you into helping us? Not that my sisters or I mind it." His brown eyes had drawn her in again.

"My mom owed him a favor." He couldn't have been more grateful that she had—and that he had a break during the construction season.

"Ah."

As she entered his name and number into her contacts, she realized that once he and his uncle left, she and her sisters wouldn't have a way to get around. They could ask Ms. Cecilia if they could borrow her car, but since she had said she would be staying with her sister, that didn't seem likely.

"Um, Nick?" She bit her lip.

"Yeah?" She made him want to kiss her.

"My sisters and I don't have a way to get around. We could probably call a cab, but I was wondering if you could help us out with that."

"Yeah, sure. I guess."

"Thank you so much!" She immediately hugged him.

Letting go of him, Nick was about to lean in for a kiss when her sisters and Ms. Cecilia came back into the parlor, interrupting their moment.

CHAPTER 6

"Ms. Cecilia's going to take us to get some dinner before heading over to her sister's," Sarah announced, completely oblivious to Jessica and Nick's interest in each other.

Immediately distancing themselves from each other, Jessica thanked God that they hadn't walked in on him kissing her.

"Sounds good. And Nick said he wouldn't mind being our chauffeur while we're here."

"I'm sure he wouldn't—at least not yours," Melissa muttered. She realized that they were too hasty in returning to the parlor. Had they waited just a couple of minutes more, Jessica would've gotten her kiss with time to spare.

"Well, my uncle's probably wondering what's taking me so long." Nick looked at them and then Jessica. The desire to kiss her was now all he could think about.

Thanking Nick for bringing their bags in, the sisters said goodbye. After watching him close the front door behind him, they soon heard the sound of Detective Murray's car leaving their aunt and uncle's house.

Grabbing their bags and taking them upstairs, Sarah took her uncle and aunt's room, Melissa took the maid's bedroom, and Jessica claimed the guest bedroom.

Leaving her suitcase on the bed for unpacking later, Melissa went into Jessica's room. "Sorry we interrupted your chance at Nick kissing you."

"It's not a big deal. I'll have to call him tomorrow so he can take us grocery shopping, so I'll definitely get another chance."

"Leave it to Aunt May to have her death turn into a matchmaking opportunity." Melissa shook her head at her.

"What? The man's hot—and hopefully a good kisser." She shrugged.

"Let's just go get some dinner. I'm starving!" Melissa halted Jessica's unpacking, forcing her to go downstairs with her. They joined Sarah and Ms. Cecilia to head out to dinner. On the drive to the restaurant, Jessica thought about calling Nick when they got back to their aunt and uncle's house. She wondered if he would be up for a little shopping and then going to the beach the next day.

Knowing that Sarah would take the lead in handling their aunt's service, Jessica figured a day at the beach with Nick Powell would be something her aunt May would definitely be okay with. With a smile on her face, she wondered what he looked like shirtless.

Lying on her bed after returning from dinner, Jessica took out her cell phone. She wondered what Nick sounded like on the phone. With any luck, sexy. With excitement for him possibly picking up his phone, she made sure the door was locked before dialing his number. Hearing a few rings, she began to wonder if she would have to suffice with just leaving a message. However, right as she thought she had heard the last ring before his greeting came on, she heard him pick up.

"Hello?"

"Nick?"

"Yeah, this is he. Who's calling?"

"It's Jessica. Jessica Parker."

"Ah, Jessica! Is everything all right? Did you need me to come back over there?"

"Oh, yeah. Everything's fine. I was just wondering if you would be up for some shopping tomorrow and then going to the beach afterward." She bit her lip, hoping he would say yes.

"Uh, shopping? I don't know. That's not really my thing. But I definitely wouldn't mind going to the beach with you after." He imagined her in a bikini.

"Well, the shopping is to buy a bikini. When I packed my weeks' worth of clothes, swimwear wasn't included. So you would be helping me pick out a bikini."

"Oh, well, in that case, sure." He now imagined watching her try them on.

"Great! Then we can go after you take us grocery shopping."

"What about your sisters? Won't they need my services too?"

"Ah, I'm sure Sarah can get done everything she needs to from the house. She's got a laptop and her phone."

"And Melissa?"

"Melissa wouldn't have anywhere to go."

"I guess it's a date, then."

"Yep, and then you can introduce me to the nightlife here."

"Jessica, you do remember why you and your sisters flew out here, right?"

"Nick, my aunt wouldn't want me to stop living my life. Yeah, it's tragic what happened, but I met a hot guy and she would want me to take advantage of that."

"You think I'm hot?" He grinned.

"Uh, yeah. And I wouldn't mind your coming back over here for a good night kiss." She could hear his smile.

"I wouldn't mind doing that either."

"See you soon."

Hanging up his phone, Nick liked Jessica's assertiveness. There was something hot about her already telling him what she thought and what she wanted. And those lips ... He couldn't wait to kiss those lips!

CHAPTER 7

Pulling his '65 baby blue convertible Mustang into the driveway, Nick cut the engine. He'd barely gotten out of the car and closed his door when he saw her quietly coming outside to meet him.

"Are you up past your bedtime?" he teased as he watched her signal for him to be quiet.

Taking his hand in hers, Jessica led him back into the house and out to the backyard, flipping a switch for the backyard lights.

As he came into view of the backyard's landscaping, Nick found himself impressed. The front yard had just been the start of the property's intricate design. Using the pool as its focal point, the Willards had masterfully designed a leisurely area that included a Jacuzzi with its own storage for towels and a bench for sitting, a lounge area for two that provided a place for simply soaking in the sun or reading a book, and a table in between for drinks and snacks. Surrounding the well-thought-out layout were more greenery and flowers. May Willard loved her flowers.

"So what do you think?" She took a moment to take in the feel of his hand in hers. She could feel the electricity from his touch.

The glow of the backyard lights made the moment even more romantic.

"I think I'm glad I came back over." He smiled.

"Me too."

Bringing her into his arms, Nick closed the gap between them and kissed her lips. "We won't have to worry about anyone interrupting us this time, will we?" he asked as he kept her in his arms.

"Nope. Both Melissa and Sarah have gone to bed, and Ms. Cecilia left after dropping us off after dinner."

Smiling, he returned his lips to hers. Enjoying the softness of them, he took the kiss a little deeper.

"Hmm, you're going to get me in trouble. I'm not a one-night-stand type of girl, but I wouldn't mind making out with you for the rest of it."

"Don't you think your sisters would hear us?"

"We could sleep out here."

"That sounds doable."

"I'll go grab the comforter, then."

Watching her disappear back into the house, Nick realized he was going to owe his uncle big time for getting to meet Jessica. Her spontaneous nature was sexy, and oh, those lips! Now that he'd had a taste of them, he wanted more.

Taking a seat on one of the loungers and stretching out his legs, Nick got comfortable as he waited for her return. Minutes later, she was reopening the back door and joining him on it.

Wrapped in his arms and covered by the guest bed's comforter, Jessica got to know Nick on a much more intimate level. Every now and then, they'd share another kiss, and the warmth of his body against hers made her so glad she had asked him to come over.

"Do you think your sisters will be surprised to see me with you like this?"

"Melissa won't. She already knows I'm into you. Sarah, on the other hand, will. She has no idea about my interest in you."

"You only told one sister about your interest in me?"

"Actually, Melissa figured it out early on when we met at the airport."

"Ah."

"She teased me about accidentally getting your attention on the drive over here."

"I will admit that I did have to force myself not to look back at you."

Giving him a kiss for his sweet sentiment, Jessica wondered if they could last past the week.

"So, what do you think your aunt would say about your being this way with me so fast?"

"That she would be happy for me. She was all about seizing the day."

"You don't think she would tell you we're rushing this?" he asked with raised eyebrows.

"Nope. She and I were kindred spirits in that way. She showed me that it's okay to go after what you want, regardless of what others think."

"I think I would've liked her." He brought her into another kiss.

"I think she would've liked you too." She returned it with one more before falling asleep in his arms.

CHAPTER 8

Waking up in Nick's arms, Jessica wondered if she would be able to sneak him up to the guest bedroom without waking her sisters. After all, since they would just be sleeping, being able to curl up in the bed with him would be a whole lot more comfortable than the restrictiveness of the lounger.

Gently coaxing him awake with a kiss, Jessica quietly led him to the guest bedroom. After putting the comforter back on the bed, she locked the door.

Taking off his shoes, Nick crawled into the bed. Watching Jessica remove her bra from under her shirt and change her jeans to pajama pants, made him smile. He liked that she was tastefully uninhibited around him.

After making herself more comfortable, Jessica joined him in the bed. Once again held in his arms, they went back to sleep. Hours later, they woke to the sound of her sisters beginning their day.

"Good morning." Jessica kissed him.

"Good morning back." He ran a hand through her bed hair. "I'm thinking we should start making this sleepover thing a regular occurrence." He loved the feel of her soft auburn hair against his skin as her light green eyes captivated him.

"Even though it doesn't include sex?" Jessica once again wondered what he looked like with his shirt off.

"I'm still in bed with you, aren't I?"

Smiling, she returned to kissing him. "I definitely wouldn't mind sharing the guest bed with you until I leave."

"Then we'll have to talk about what we're going to do after that because I don't want this to end." He slid a hand under her shirt and caressed her side.

Nick was entranced by her. Just the feel of her body in his arms as they slept had felt so comfortable to him.

"Me either."

Just the fact that he wasn't trying to get away with sliding his hand up her body any farther made a huge impression on her. Nick was a very respectful guy. Even after leading him into her bed, the only thing he took off were his shoes.

"Will your sisters mind if I start sleeping over?" Nick began putting his shoes back on.

"I can let them know, but other than that, it's my choice if I have someone in this bed with me."

"True, but this is also your aunt and uncle's house. So I want to remain respectful of that."

She straddled him once he finished with both of his shoes. "I think it's hot that you're so considerate."

Smiling, he kissed her. "And I think it's time we headed downstairs for breakfast."

"Assuming there is food for breakfast."

"If not, I have my car."

"Yes, you do."

After making a detour for the bathroom, Jessica showed up in the kitchen with her surprise guest.

"Nick," Sarah greeted while Melissa poured coffee. Taking in his bed head and clothes from the day before, she wondered just how much sleeping he and her sister had actually done.

"Good morning." He accepted a cup.

"Are you ready to be our chauffeur while we're here?" Melissa teased. Glancing from him to Jessica, she could tell their chemistry was strong.

"Sure. Wherever you need to go."

"Sounds good to me. Jessica, this one's a keeper," Melissa replied. She lifted her cup to him as she left the kitchen.

"Melissa and I have already had breakfast. Ms. Cecilia said that she had gone grocery shopping right before Aunt May's death. However, she only bought what Aunt May would've eaten, so we'll need to head back to the grocery store to get what we want. Will you be okay with taking us to the grocery store like that or did you want to head home and change first?" Sarah asked Nick.

"Honestly, it's whatever you three would prefer. I can stay in the car while you're in there."

"Okay, then I'll start making a list," Sarah easily agreed, leaving Nick and Jessica the kitchen.

"I think that means both your sisters like me." He put down his coffee cup and pulled her into his arms.

"You questioned that?" Jessica wrapped her arms around his neck.

"Jessica, I'm more than just driving the three of you around now—of course I'm going to question that."

"Then it's a damn good thing they do." She accepted the invitation to run her fingers through his hair before kissing him.

CHAPTER 9

"Cecilia, do we even know if the sisters know anything about their aunt and uncle's true worth?" her husband, Damon, asked her.

"I don't think they have a clue. I think George and May kept their finances a secret from everyone. Besides the prominent persona she put forth, no one really knows where they stood financially—aside from being rich, of course."

"Huh. Well, my uncle Gino suspects that George Willard had some hidden financial endeavors that turned out to be rather successful, so the money's there. We just have to find it."

"But, Damon, even if we find their gold mine, we've still got the sisters and their mother to contend with."

"Not if we ensure that the sisters never return to New York City. And as for their mother, well, we can figure out a way to frame her for their deaths."

"The woman's in a mental institution. How in the world would that work?"

"Cecilia, we'll figure it out. Our primary goal right now is to find the money. Then we'll make the Parker sisters disappear."

Cecilia felt bad for conning May's nieces, but then again, when she had found out her true fortune, she'd wanted a piece of it. After all, she'd given the woman over a decade of service so she deserved to be well compensated for it.

"All right. The whole thing just makes me uneasy. What if the girls somehow find out?"

"You said it has been years since they'd had any communication between them, right?"

"Yes. The day May's sister was admitted to the mental institution, all communication between the girls and their aunt completely stopped. It broke May's heart. For whatever reason, their father ceased them from having a relationship with her."

"That's too bad for them, but good for us."

The girls would have no family support while they were here. Sure, they could call their father if they needed help, but he lived on the opposite coast. Hell, their relationship with their father might've gone south too. Damon had no idea the amount of luck the sisters' poor family situation might give him and Cecilia.

Returning to the guest bedroom after breakfast, Nick waited for Jessica and her sisters to get ready to go to the grocery store. Taking a seat on the bed, he watched Jessica prepare for the day.

"Should I bring over some clothes to sleep in after our date?"

"If you want to, I guess." Jessica picked out the day's clothes.

"Well, they would be a whole lot more comfortable than my jeans."

"Nick, bring over what you want to bring over, though you'll probably want to head home for showers and changing clothes."

"You mean I can't just share your shower?" Teasing, he stopped what she was doing and pulled her to him.

"No! If we're not having sex yet, then you definitely can't take a shower with me. Nick, I do have my standards."

"Yet?"

His grin caught her attention. "Well, of course. I mean, don't you want to at some point?" She looked at him with concern.

"The word *no* does not even fit into my vocabulary for that one."

"Then currently you're just sharing the guest bed for sleeping."

"And I'm fine with that."

"Glad to hear it. Because if you weren't, we would have a problem."

"Which means no more sleepovers."

"Yep."

"Does this mean you're waiting for marriage?"

"I don't know yet. But I am waiting until I fall in love, and I know I'm ready."

"Then I like your standards."

"Me too. Besides, I know my sisters would find it extremely uncomfortable if they accidentally walked into the bathroom while you were in the shower or saw you shirtless while you were getting ready for the day."

"Yeah, I can see how that would be a bit unnerving for them." He thought for a moment. "Though I like the idea of playing house with you."

"Maybe one day it just might get to happen." She smiled with a mischievous twinkle in her eyes.

Giving her a kiss, Nick let her finish getting ready.

Realizing that it would probably take a while for all three girls to be ready to go, Nick let Sarah know that he had changed his mind about heading home to change clothes.

CHAPTER 10

Hearing Nick's car return to the house, Jessica found herself already missing him. He'd only been gone a few hours, but for her heart, it'd felt like eternity. How could she be taken by a guy so deeply and so fast that his missing presence had made such an impact on her?

They had spent one romantic night together that had turned into him sharing her bed. It was just crazy to her that her heart had already become so attached to him. She wondered if they could make a long-distance relationship work once it was time for her and her sisters to head back to New York City—unless, of course, he was up for moving to the East Coast to be with her. She knew there was no way she could see herself moving so far away from her sisters.

Knocking on the door, Nick hoped the girls were ready to go.

With her heart rushing her to him, she let him inside. "Hi." She slipped her hands into his. "It's crazy, but I actually missed you, despite it only being a few hours."

Giving her a quick kiss, Nick liked the welcoming homecoming. "Are your sisters ready to go?"

"Yep. Sarah's got the list ready."

"Sounds good." Jessica's hands felt just right in his. "Should we get going, then?"

"Yeah. Sarah, Melissa, Nick is back to take us to the grocery store!"

Hearing their responses, Jessica followed Nick out to his car. Seeing the Mustang with its top down made her anxious for their time alone once they were ready to go shopping for her bikini.

As they waited for her sisters to join them, Jessica wondered if she should hold his hand during the drive. She definitely wanted to but didn't know if it would make her sisters feel uncomfortable. Then again, they might wonder why they weren't.

Being with Nick was a different experience for her. His laid-back personality fit her free-spirited vibe easily, but his considerate nature was what really got her attention. She had dated a string of guys who matched her easygoing disposition, but the rest of their personalities just never intrigued her. She'd never felt that heartstring pull that Nick had caused from being out of her eyesight for just mere hours.

Moments later, Sarah and Melissa joined them in getting into the car. Leaving the front seat for Jessica, they climbed into the back.

After putting on her seat belt, Jessica watched Nick to see if he would show his desire to hold her hand. Sure enough, after leaving her aunt and uncle's house, he naturally slipped his hand into hers. Feeling his skin against hers made her smile and brought a warmth to her heart. It was safe to say she was already falling in love with the guy.

Despite previously telling Sarah that he would probably just stay in the car the whole time, Nick ended up going inside with them and learning Jessica's tastes in food. He thought about the two of them picking out food for a picnic while they were at the beach but then changed his mind when he realized that he had no idea how long their shopping trip would take. Taking her out to dinner after the beach would end up having to be the trade-off.

"Damon, you're going to have to make this quick. I don't want any of the Willards' neighbors getting suspicious," his uncle warned.

Sitting in his uncle's car, Damon prepared to break into their house. With the car parked in front of another neighbor's house, Damon slipped on a pair of black gloves. "Don't worry—I will."

Getting out of the car, he put his hands into his pockets as he walked to their property. Thankful that no one else was around and that there were very few cars in driveways or parked along the curb, he tried to remain as unassuming as possible. Once at the Willards' front door, he jimmied it open and went inside. Intending only to scare the sisters, he made the house look as if it had been ransacked.

With the house now a mess, he left the front door only slightly closed and returned to his uncle's car.

CHAPTER 11

Returning to the house with the convertible's trunk packed full of groceries, Sarah put the key Ms. Cecilia had given her into the lock. But as she turned the key, they watched it easily open.

"Girls, stay out here!" Nick immediately directed.

Not questioning his order, they watched him cautiously open the door as he entered the house.

As he examined the house's interior, he was welcomed to the sight of Damon's staged mess. Going through each room, it looked like nothing had been left untouched; even the girls' clothes had been scattered on the floor. Seeing mess after mess, he began to wonder who had broken into their aunt and uncle's house, why they had, and whether they took anything.

Given that he was just a guest, there was no possible way he could answer his last question. As for the girls, they might be able to depending on how well they knew their aunt or if any of their own stuff had been stolen.

"Okay, it's all clear. You girls are safe to enter your aunt and uncle's house now," Nick announced, coming down the stairs. "I'm going to call my uncle to let him know what happened."

Taking out his phone, Nick speed-dialed his uncle's number as the girls took in the extent of the mess. Hearing him update his uncle on the intrusion, the girls began putting things back and throwing away anything that had been damaged in the process.

"Okay, my uncle's up to speed. Do you girls know if anything's been taken?" He slipped his phone back into his pocket.

After hearing a resounding no, he headed back to his car and began bringing in the groceries. With the downstairs looking more back to normal, the girls halted cleaning and helped Nick.

"Guess I'm glad you're now sleeping over," Jessica whispered as she grabbed more groceries from the car.

"Hell, at this point, my uncle would've insisted that I crash on the couch." He put a hand on her left hip.

"And instead, you get to share the nice warm guest bed with me." She gave him a kiss before taking the bags inside.

Nick wondered how long he could share her bed before his desire to be closer to her ended his ability to just sleep next to her. Even though he'd originally told her that he'd be fine with not having sex, the more he was around her, the more he began questioning that.

Closing the trunk and locking the car, Nick returned to the kitchen. "Do you girls know if your aunt and uncle had any enemies?"

"No, not really. After we stopped keeping in touch with them, who knows who she might've had an issue with at one time or another?" Sarah answered for them as she put the groceries away.

"Huh. And her maid, Ms. Cecilia, was never harboring any feelings of resentment toward her?"

"Taking after your uncle, I see." Sarah smirked.

"I just want to make sure you three stay safe while you're here. That's all." He shrugged, though with a more concentrated look at Jessica.

"And we appreciate that—we really do. But there's no one. If there were, we would tell you." Sarah ended it, putting away the last of the groceries.

Melissa changed the subject. "So, what do you and Jessica have planned for today?"

"He's taking me bikini shopping and then we're going to the beach."

"Good luck with that one." Melissa patted Nick's arm on her way out of the kitchen.

"Jessica, tomorrow I thought we'd start looking into if Aunt May had a will before we begin planning anything," Sarah said. "Nick,

I'll let you know if we'll need your chauffeuring services again. We really appreciate your taking the time to help us."

Nodding, Jessica remembered that Aunt May's body was still in the morgue.

Nick looked at Jessica. "I'll be around. And absolutely."

Watching Sarah leave the kitchen and head upstairs, he turned to Jessica. "You ready to go shopping for a bikini?"

"I think you're more excited about that than I am."

"I'm excited to see you in one." He came up behind her, wrapping her in his arms. "I think you're hot too." He kissed her neck.

CHAPTER 12

Showing her some of the Bay Area, Nick drove to the local mall, where they found a PacSun store. Sifting through different bikini styles, Jessica began her hunt for a new bikini.

As she was trying on bikini after bikini, Nick just watched with enjoyment as each one accentuated Jessica's curves. But as he saw more of her skin, it made him seriously question his ability to just sleep next to her when they went to bed that night.

"Okay, I think I've decided," she declared.

Coming out of the dressing room fully dressed and with a selection of bikinis in her hand, she had changed her mind about buying just one.

"What's the verdict?"

"I think I just want to splurge, so I'm going to get a few of them."

"Well, you looked hot in each one, so you definitely can't go wrong with any of them."

"Did you need to buy some board shorts or are you good?" She slid her free hand under his shirt and felt his abs. They felt tight, and his body felt fit.

"Getting a head start, I see." Nick smiled.

"I'm just curious to see what you look like with your shirt off."

"Well then, hurry up and buy those bikinis and I'll show you."

She removed her hand from his skin. "Sounds good to me."

With a new assortment of bikinis to wear, Jessica headed back to the convertible with Nick. Holding his hand to and from the store had left her feeling as if they had been a couple for years.

"I'm going to make a detour to my house so we can change for the beach and I can get us some towels and sunscreen."

"Already bringing me home?" She gave him a teasing smile.

"Relax, Jessica. I live alone. You won't be meeting my parents." He shook his head at her humor.

Driving to his house, Nick kept the convertible's top down, as the clear sky gave them a perfect day. Glancing at Jessica, he couldn't help but feel as if he had fallen for her. Just from the way she looked, to the smile she shot him every so often, he couldn't imagine spending the day with anyone else. He had absolutely no idea how he was truly going to thank his uncle for asking him to tag along with him to the airport.

Unlocking the door to his place, Nick directed Jessica to the bathroom. Heading into his bedroom, he readied himself for the beach. Grabbing two beach towels from the closet, and sunscreen from a bathroom drawer, he knocked on the guest bathroom door.

"Are you ready to go?"

She opened the door. "Yep." Seeing the change in his appearance, Jessica liked what she saw. "Can I get a tour of your place first?"

"Uh, sure."

He guided her around to each area of his house. When they reached his bedroom, she sat down on his bed.

"Maybe the next time I come to California, we could have a sleepover here."

Smirking, he said, "I don't think that would be such a good idea." He continued leaning against the doorway.

"Why not?"

"Because, Jessica, without your sisters here, we wouldn't get much sleep."

He pushed back the urge to join her on the bed.

"Then I guess that means I'll have to wait a good amount of time before I come back here."

Getting off the bed, Jessica walked over to him slowly. Bringing him into a sensuous kiss with her left hand around the back of his neck, she let him know exactly how she felt about him.

"Then I can't wait to share my bed with you."

Smiling, Jessica led him back out to his car, only stopping for him to lock the front door. "To the beach, chauffeur!" She waited for him to open her door for her before getting in.

"My pleasure." He slipped his hand back into hers.

When they neared the beach, they could instantly smell the salt water. But as Nick found a place to park, he found himself more anxious to see Jessica in one of her bikinis than the beach itself.

Gathering the towels and sunscreen, they headed for the sand.

"How long do we want to stay here?" Jessica asked once they had found a place to lay down their towels.

Looking around, it was practically secluded. Their only company were a few seagulls keeping watch and some other beachgoers a ways down.

Taking off her outer clothes, she revealed her chosen bikini to him—a floral design, with various shades of blue, in honor of her aunt.

"As long as you want. I figured that once we've had enough, I'd take you to dinner." He stripped down to his board shorts.

"Really? And where would you want to take me?" She smiled.

Gazing at every muscle in his upper body, Jessica was impressed. His biceps showed her the strength he had built up in his upper arms, and his torso showed off the effect his construction work had had on his muscles. Nick Powell had a hot body!

"Where would you like to go?" Grabbing the sunscreen, he started spreading it on himself.

"Any place that serves a really good cheeseburger," she answered as she waited her turn for the sunscreen.

Handing it to her once he was finished, he said, "I'm sure I can find a place using my phone."

"Will I want to go back to my aunt and uncle's house and change first?"

Realizing that he still needed his back and neck covered, she easily did the honors. Just running her hands all over his skin made her anticipate him returning the favor.

"That all depends on how fancy you want the restaurant to be. After all, this is our first date, so it's up to you."

"Hmm, so I could have you dress up in a suit and tie and see how sexy you look that way. Or I could have us keep it causal and just have you with a freshly showered look? You've given me a lot to think about, Nick."

Thinking about it as she worked on spreading the sunscreen all over her skin, she gave the sunscreen back to him for him to cover her back and neck.

"Sounds like a no-lose situation for you," he teased as he began spreading it all over her back.

"It does, doesn't it?"

However, as she felt his hands spread the sunscreen over her skin, she got a better idea. "Would you mind doing that while I lie down?"

Smiling, he replied, "Nope. Not at all."

He watched her get comfortable on the towel before reaching back and unhooking her bikini top.

"There, now I won't have tan lines and you won't have to work your hands around the material."

"You just wanted me to give you a back massage." He easily complied.

"And I very much appreciate it." She blew him a kiss as a thank-you. "It even makes this the best first date I've ever been on."

She said with a grin, "I'm glad you're enjoying it."

Taking in her soft skin, he watched her body instantly relax. Finishing her massage not long after, Nick moved back to his beach towel. Looking out into the Bay's waves, watching them eventually come crashing into the shoreline, he had never felt more content on a date. Just looking over at Jessica and seeing how restful she looked, he would've done the whole day over again just to capture this moment.

CHAPTER 13

Returning to the car at sunset, Jessica got back into the front passenger seat while Nick put the towels and sunscreen in the trunk.

"Have you decided what you want to do for dinner?" He slid back into the driver's seat.

Taking a moment to think about his question, Jessica surprised Nick by straddling him.

"Uh, Jessica, what are you doing?"

"I just wanted to say thank you. Thank you for this date, thank you for being you, and most importantly, thank you for getting my mind off my aunt's murder. Having you to spend time with has just been such a godsend for me." She brought him into a kiss.

Feeling her put her passion into it, Nick slipped his hands under her shirt and caressed her skin.

She was glad they were alone, with no one in sight. As the kissing heated up, she could feel herself naturally grind up against him.

She whispered into his ear as his hands made her body feel even hotter. "Put the top up."

Part of him wanted to obey her command as he watched her slip off her top to expose her bikini top to him. But as she stripped away her clothes to be closer to him, he began to question if what they were doing was right. Sex was the destination, but the question was whether she was truly ready or if this passionate explosion of affection was really just her way of dealing with her aunt's death.

"I want you, Nick ... more than I've ever wanted any guy!" she whispered in his ear. She took off his shirt, sliding her hands up his torso as she did it. "I know it's my first time, but I don't care."

Hearing her confession, Nick relented on putting the top up. "Jessica, we can't."

Despite his objection to her clear desire, her continual grinding made it hard for him to stop being turned on, and just the way her voice sounded in his ear, they weren't just heading in the direction of sex, they were barreling toward it.

Like the waves crashing on the beach in front of them, Jessica's grinding came to a crashing halt. Slowly she opened her eyes and left the comfort of his lips.

"I'm sorry," he heard in the quietest of whispers. Had she not been inches away from him, he wouldn't have heard it.

"It's okay. I get. Believe me, I do. But sex is not going to take away your pain."

As he stared into her eyes, looking for confirmation of his words, he realized that she had been thinking about having sex with him the moment they got back into his car. That's what her silence had been about.

Feeling his heart rate go back down as the level of heat between them slowly faded away, he searched her eyes for a response. He watched a tear slowly make its way down her soft face. It was clear to him that sex was her means of dealing with her aunt's death.

As Jessica looked back into Nick's eyes, she could see the compassion he felt for her. It was enough to push her to release the grief she felt. First one tear and then another. Soon her vision became blurry and Nick was pulling her against him, letting the comfort of his closeness help heal her sadness.

Forgoing the sex she thought she desired, Jessica let go and let her tears cleanse her from her grief. As she felt Nick's comforting arms around her, with his hands bringing warmth to her back, she felt a sense of security she had never known before.

Nick could have easily followed her desire, and instead of her grieving her aunt's death with her tears, they could be having sex right now. Instead, he had been selfless. He had redirected her fleshly desire and shown her what she truly needed. Nick Powell was the ultimate compliment to her personality. She would never find a better match for herself.

"Thank you," she whispered. Her tear-stained face told him just how much she had needed his comfort.

"You're welcome, Jess." He smiled.

She was beautiful to him. Just the way her body felt in his arms, Nick found himself awestruck by her. As much as he would've loved experiencing the intimacy that sex would have given them, with her, holding her in his arms felt more natural to him than anything he'd ever experienced in his life. Jessica was it for him. She was his dream girl brought to life.

"Jess. You're the first guy to call me that." She thought about the new intimacy it brought to them. "I think I like it." She gave him a quick kiss.

"I'm sorry you can't shorten my nickname anymore." He gave her a teasing smile.

"Funny." She played with his hair. "Nick, I'm sorry I pushed you so much." She remembered the feeling of his member hardening underneath her. "I guess I was just tired of feeling the pain. Kissing you and feeling your hands slide all over my skin just made me feel like my world was perfect again, like the reason for my trip to California no longer existed and any sadness I've felt from my family's demise was just long gone."

"And under different circumstances, I wouldn't have stopped it. But right now I don't want your first time to be from the result of your grief."

"You sound like you have some experience."

"Well, when my dad died from a construction accident years ago, I needed to find a way to deal with my grief. I went from one relationship to another, but the grief never subsided. Finally, my mom insisted I go to church with her one Sunday, and that helped a lot. It showed me that only God heals and that it's a day-by-day process."

"So does that mean you tried to use sex to end your grief?" She raised her eyebrows.

"No. It means that I would get close to it but then stop it before we reached that point."

"So, you're a virgin too?"

"Yes, I am."

"Are you waiting for marriage as well?"

He smiled. "Jess, I'm waiting for the right woman."

"Does that mean you think I'm her, considering that any more grinding and I would be sitting on your lap completely naked right now, having sex with you?"

Curiosity for what her body looked like naked drifted through his mind. "What if you are? What would you say to that?" He knew she was completely right.

"I would say that it's very possible. As much as my aunt was a free spirit, she was also very well aware that my uncle was the only man for her. She was never one to wander from relationship to relationship. She simply knew what she wanted and stayed the path."

"What do you think she would say about us, about this?"

"I think she would've appreciated your willingness to stop me from using my grief as an excuse." She understood the importance of that connection and the reason it shouldn't be used other than as a way to express one's love for the other person.

"You do make it damn hard for me to not want to continue."

Giving him a kiss, she teased his mouth with her tongue.

"I think I love you," he softly added with a smile.

"Just because I know how to kiss you?" she teased back.

"No, but I do like that. It's because of how you make me feel. Jessica, I love that a simple kiss from your lips can turn me on. That your spirited personality makes me feel more alive than I've ever felt before. And the way you love your family shows me how you'd love me and our kids, if we have kids. Deep and strong."

"And all from just a first date?"

"We did talk pretty late into the night when you asked me to come over and give you a good night kiss."

"True." She gave him another quick kiss. "I enjoyed being so close to you as we lay on that lounge chair wrapped up in each other's arms."

Smiling, he returned it. He let his kiss do the talking as he pulled her back into their sexual chemistry. Just feeling her lips against his kept his desire fueled. They didn't need to do anything beyond kissing. The passion behind their attraction for each other maintained the intensity of their kiss.

"Hmm, you know how to make it hot in your car." She licked her lips once he allowed her to breathe.

"It takes two for that one, Jess." He winked.

Unable to keep from smiling, she grabbed her shirt and slipped it back on. "By the way, I think I love you too." She gave him one last quick kiss before getting back into the passenger seat.

CHAPTER 14

Looking over at her with her shirt back on and her seat belt buckled, Nick prepared to start the car. Turning on the defroster, he waited while the car cleared their built-up heat from the windows.

"Nick?" Jessica turned to him. His shirt was covering the skin where her hands had once been.

"Yeah?" He pulled out his phone to look up nearby restaurants that served burgers.

"If we'd had sex, would that've changed what's between us?" Her thoughts went back to reality now that the heat between them had vanished.

"In what way? Jess, we just admitted to each other that we think we love each other."

"I know. But what are we going to do when I have to head back to New York City with my sisters? Are we feeling this way only because I'm grieving my aunt's death, and once the shock is over with, we won't necessarily feel the same?"

Nick paused his scrolling and gave her his full attention. "Jess, my love for you is not a result of the situation with your aunt's murder. Hell, if anything, your aunt's murder is what brought us together."

"I know it's how we met. But say we do actually have sex? What then? I don't want to have sex with you only to have to head back home and never see you again."

"Jess, we'll figure it out." He slipped his hand into hers. "And I don't want that either. When we have sex, it's not just going to be for a hookup. When I have sex with you, there's going to be a permanency to our relationship."

"A permanency?"

"Yes."

"But wouldn't that mean marriage?"

"It can—if you want it to. I have no problem making this the last first date I ever go on." He smiled.

"But, Nick, that would mean you will have already fallen in love with me. We haven't known each other long enough, or well enough, to be at that point yet."

"Maybe not, but that doesn't mean we won't both decide that once we do get to that point." He took in her shocked expression. "When I told you I love you, my statement wasn't void of the truth. I meant it."

"I know you did. I guess this is just something so different for me. I've never met a guy who's made me feel this way before, and I think at some point, I probably will fall in love with you."

"Glad to hear it. Now, how about we go get some dinner to finish this eventful night?"

"That's sounds good. I'm starving, now that you mention it." She put a hand to her belly as she heard it growl.

"I suppose kissing can create quite an appetite." He gave her a teasing smile as he picked a restaurant from his phone.

Shaking her head at him, she said, "Jessica Powell. Mrs. Jessica Powell."

"My last name sounds good with yours, doesn't it?" He smiled.

"Wow, Nick! I can't believe we're already talking marriage."

"Saying I love you and talking about marriage—is that too much for a first date?" He laughed. "If you want, I can ask my mom for my grandmother's ring." He looked down at her left ring finger. As much as he was teasing her, he could also envision himself putting it on her finger.

Jessica looked down at her left hand, imagining a ring on it. "I know you think it's funny, but it's something I'm seriously considering. My aunt May met my uncle George when she was about my age. Although they'd only known each other for a couple of weeks before marrying, somehow my aunt knew that he was the one for her."

"Your uncle George probably knew the same, then." The seriousness in his tone came back. He would've asked her the question right there but realized that he didn't want his engagement to include his board shorts and no ring to put on her finger.

"Nick, do you think that what we experienced at the airport with each other was love at first sight?" The thought hit her like an aha moment.

"It very well could be. I mean, it's one thing to have such a strong connection with someone, but to pair that with love ... I think the only way we could truly know is to test it."

"Are you saying you want to try a long-distance relationship? Because that's what that means once my aunt's murder has been solved and we've given her a proper goodbye."

"Stay."

"What?"

"Stay, Jessica. Don't go back to New York City with your sisters. Stay here with me."

"But, Nick—"

"Jessica, we can do this. We can make us work."

"You're asking a lot of me."

"I know, but that's what I want. I want you to stay in California and be with me."

Taking a deep breath, she said, "Okay."

As Jessica thought about what life would be like once she and her sisters returned to New York City, she realized that it would only allow her to have a lot of phone calls and video chatting between her and Nick, and that wasn't enough. She would crave to see him in person. Every day it would be a longing that wouldn't be satisfied until either she made the trip out to California again or he came to visit her. It meant she wouldn't get the luxury of being held in his arms when she desired his affection.

"Okay?"

"Okay. I will." She briskly nodded.

"Do you think Sarah and Melissa are going to be okay with your staying?"

"They'll have to be."

"And what about you? Will you be okay with not going back with them?"

"Nick, you had me on your hook at the airport the second I looked into your eyes. I'll have to be."

Giving her a kiss for the sentiment, he drove them to the restaurant he had chosen.

After being seated in a booth, Jessica looked at her hand and began to imagine the ring on her finger.

"I'll still need to ask you first." He grinned, picking up the menu.

"I know. I just like to imagine what it'll be like to actually have a ring on that finger."

"How about you first figure out what you want to eat and then you can imagine away?"

"Ah, a lifetime of your teasing."

"Or a lifetime of our getting to know each other like we were about to in my convertible."

With wide eyes, all she could do was shake her head at him.

"Trust me, Jessica. Marrying me will be the best adventure you will ever go on." He offered his hand to her.

"And I can't wait, once you pop the question, of course." She easily accepted it.

Returning to his convertible once dinner was over, Nick looked at Jessica, thoughtfully slipping his hand into hers. "Jess ..."

Taking a moment to appreciate her, knowing that at some point down the road he would ask her to marry him, he took in her beauty. But as he flashed back to her straddling him, he took in the significance of their closeness. The realization hit him hard.

She wasn't just another relationship for him. She would become his wife.

"Yeah?" She looked over at him. "I think my sisters are going to find your new nickname for me cute."

He gave her a sexy grin. "You should know that I want to pursue a relationship with you the right way. I don't want to rush into anything. I want us to continue to take our time in getting to know each other."

"So no more spontaneous almost sex, then? Is that what you mean?" she teased when their eyes connected.

Jessica couldn't help but laugh at herself. She had hurriedly straddled his lap and was about ready to take off her bikini top as she turned him on, but he stopped them from having sex. She had never done anything even close to that before in her life.

"Jessica, you surprise me."

Her questioning look made him realize that he'd given her an answer she wasn't expecting. "I love your spontaneity. I've never dated a woman who was just so open with herself like you are. I've also never had the kind of connection with a girlfriend that I clearly have with you."

Jessica shifted her body to face him. She enjoyed seeing this softer side to him. "Go on," she teased.

"Funny. But I'm serious. I love the excitement you bring to my life. Jess, the way we fit together just feels so perfect." He leaned over and gave her a kiss.

His words made her feel relaxed. "Just wait until we do actually have sex. I bet I'll blow your mind!" she teased again.

"I'm sure you will." He chuckled at her sentiment. "I just love knowing that everything feels so natural with you. From that spark we first felt to the fire we let burn earlier tonight, it has never been work getting us there."

"I guess it's a good thing you plan to ask me to marry you at some point?"

"It damn sure is!" He fired up his convertible's engine and drove them back to her aunt and uncle's house.

CHAPTER 15

"This is Detective Murray." Sarah was greeted by his voice after using his business card to call him.

"Hello, Detective. How is my aunt's investigation going?"

"Unfortunately, we have no leads as of right now, but it is an active investigation so don't give up hope."

"Thank you, Detective. My sisters and I will try not to." She glanced at Melissa.

"Sounds good. Also, I've just received word that the examiner is finished with your aunt's body. We got the toxicology report back. There was nothing found in her system, so at least we know she wasn't under the influence of anything prior to asphyxiation."

"Thank you. I'll let my sisters know." Sarah grimaced at the thought.

She could just imagine the fear her aunt must've felt as the life was brutally taken out of her.

Hanging up, Sarah realized that she and her sisters would soon have to face the reason for their trip. Up until this point, their visit had felt more like a bittersweet homecoming, not a heartbreaking final goodbye to their beloved aunt.

"Detective Murray said that the medical examiner's finished with Aunt May. We can go see her now."

"Jessica and Nick should be back from their date soon; she'll probably want Nick to come with us," Melissa added. Melissa's throat felt dry as she pictured seeing her aunt's dead body.

"Then it's a good thing he'll already be driving us there." Sarah hugged her. "We will get through this; we always do."

Crying over the realization that her aunt was actually dead hit Melissa hard. She knew that at some point, they would have to go see her body in the morgue, but the knowledge of it had just remained a thought. It wasn't until Detective Murray's call that the thought was now a reality. "I sure hope Jessica's first date with Nick was good enough that it'll overshadow this reminder for her," Melissa tearfully added. She pictured her sister's face drenched in tears the second the reality hit her as well.

"It makes me glad she met Nick. She'll appreciate having him for support," Sarah agreed.

As the two sisters commiserated in their loss, they heard the sound of a car's tires squealing as it came to a stop in their aunt and uncle's driveway.

Wondering if that meant Jessica and Nick were now back, they broke from their embrace to head downstairs.

Opening the front door to see what the rush back had been about, they watched Ms. Cecilia get out of her car screaming, only to be shot seconds later. As her body fell to the ground, Sarah and Melissa looked at each other in total shock.

Did that really just happen? Did I really just watch my aunt's maid get shot right in front of me? What the heck is going on? Melissa's mind raced. Sarah had already left her side to see if she was still alive.

Seeing the pool of blood gathering from her torso, Sarah yelled at Melissa to go call 911 while she did her best to keep pressure on the wound.

Still in shock, and trying to process the scene in front of her, it was as if the mute button had been pressed as she watched Sarah mouth the words to her.

Fortunately, only seconds later, Nick and Jessica pulled into the driveway. With his convertible's headlights shining on the crime scene, Nick immediately parked his car. Flinging open the door, he took out his cell phone and called 911 as he rounded the car to see what had happened.

Handing his phone to Sarah so she could tell the operator what she and Melissa had witnessed, Nick borrowed Jessica's cell phone to call his uncle.

With his uncle informed and an ambulance on its way, Nick held Jessica against him.

"Is she still alive?" Melissa finally asked.

"Yes, but just barely," Sarah answered.

Sarah couldn't help but wonder what was going on. First their aunt and uncle's house was made to look as if it had been robbed, and now someone had attempted to murder their aunt's maid in the driveway. It was clear someone was sending her and her sisters a message. The questions were, *who* and *why*?

CHAPTER 16

Seeing the ambulance pull up minutes later, the four watched a paramedic check Ms. Cecilia's pulse before getting help lifting her onto a gurney. While the paramedics slid her into the ambulance as they did what they could to keep her alive, another paramedic questioned Sarah and Melissa about what had happened.

Knowing they had no information to give, Nick turned off his car and Jessica grabbed her bikinis before heading into the house.

"Who did my aunt's maid know that would want to attempt to kill her?" Jessica led Nick up to the guest room to put away her bikinis.

"I guess that's something you and your sisters now have to figure out." He took a seat on the bed.

"Don't you mean your uncle? After all, he's the detective."

"Jessica, she was your aunt's maid. Wouldn't you want to know that for yourself?"

"Nick, I have no connections in this state. How in the world could my sisters or I investigate something like this? Keep in mind that none of us knew who she was close friends with, much less anyone she ever kept in touch with over the years."

"And I realize that." He once again pulled her to him once she had finished putting her stuff away.

"Besides, we would have no idea who to start with."

"Okay, I get it. No doing your own undercover work."

"Were you hoping I would so you could get a little practice in yourself?" She ran a hand through his hair. She enjoyed the feel of it, and he had enough hair that her fingers could easily disappear within its thickness.

"Are you asking if I want to be a detective like my uncle?"

"Yeah, I guess. When we get married, I would like my husband to have career goals."

He liked her referring to him as her husband. "And you would be okay with my doing undercover work or putting my life on the line? Because that's what my uncle's job has entailed over the years."

Taking a moment to think about it, she said, "Okay, so maybe being a detective won't be in your future. Construction work keeps you in shape, so let's just stick with that." She sat down on his right leg and kissed him.

With an arm supporting her, they enjoyed basking in their affection for each other, stopping when they heard a knock.

Sarah broke off their affection. "I just wanted to let you know that Ms. Cecilia is on her way to the hospital. Nick, Melissa and I were wondering if you could give us a ride over there since her car is now a part of a crime scene."

"Sure, of course." He easily nodded.

Jessica was about to stand up to let him up when Sarah stopped her. "Jessica, hold on. You will probably want Nick's support once you hear the rest of what I have to tell you."

Looking at her in confusion, Jessica let her continue.

As she listened to Sarah paraphrase her conversation with Detective Murray regarding their aunt's body, it was all Jessica could do to not fall apart.

Feeling Jessica's body tense up at hearing that his uncle had informed the sisters that they were now able to view their aunt's body, Nick tightened his hold on her so she didn't fall to the floor.

"I thought we would go see her tomorrow. Tonight's had enough excitement already," Sarah informed them, leaving the room.

CHAPTER 17

"Nick!" Jessica crumbled into his arms. Her tears became a waterfall of emotion as reality forced itself upon her.

"I know, Jessica. I know." He pulled her completely into his arms and gently rubbed her back.

It was a reality she knew was coming, but it still hurt like hell to face it.

As Nick did his best to comfort her, Jessica was just grateful for their day together. Making love to him in his car had been a decision made out of emotional desperation. She had needed a release of her thoughts, and he had given her one. But as her emotional vacation ended, she was just glad that he was there to stick it out with her.

"Thank you for being more than just our chauffeur." Her tears emphasized her words.

"You're very welcome. Thank you for making it an easy decision, Jess." He smiled. Kissing her forehead, he cradled her against him.

"You're very welcome for that."

The drive to the medical examiner's office was silent. Even with Nick holding Jessica's hand, hers and her sisters' minds were elsewhere.

Nick found himself with the urgent need to protect Jessica and found himself wishing there was a way he could prevent her from being subjected to viewing her aunt's dead body. Unfortunately, being her support would have to suffice, and he would give her welcoming arms to be wrapped in the second she found herself unable to deal with what she saw.

"Okay, we're here." He turned off the engine.

"What?" Jessica was the only one to acknowledge him.

"I said that we're here." He let go of her hand and pointed at the medical examiner's office.

"Oh." She and her sisters unbuckled their seat belts and followed him inside.

Slipping his hand back into hers, Nick realized he could do nothing about her and her sisters' somber moods. They were about to see the dead body of a well-loved family member, and they needed to express that emotion.

After Sarah had informed the medical examiner's assistant of the reason for their visit, the four were led to a bench outside an examination room the medical examiner was currently using. As the sisters waited for the inevitable, they looked to each other for their strength. Even with Nick there as their chauffeur and to help Jessica cope, he could see their tight-knit bond.

About twenty minutes later, the medical examiner led the four to the morgue drawer that held their aunt's body. Opening the drawer and pulling out her body, the medical examiner lifted the sheet away from her face.

Immediately, Jessica buried herself in Nick's body as Melissa and Sarah trembled in each other's arms. It was true. Their aunt had been murdered, and they were now a witness to the strangulation marks around her neck.

"I'm so sorry for your loss," they heard the medical examiner say. "I'll give you all some time."

Jessica wanted it to be a lie. She wanted her aunt May's death to be a terrible practical joke, but it wasn't. The truth was as real as the marks on her neck.

"We'll have to arrange for the funeral home that handled Uncle George's funeral to transfer her remains," Sarah said with a deep breath.

This was not how Sarah had wanted to say her final goodbye to her aunt. She wanted the simple luxury of getting to say goodbye to her when she was already in her coffin and just minutes away from being lowered into the ground and buried.

"I'll help you with that." Melissa led her out of the room.

"Nick, I need you to take my mind off my aunt's murder." Jessica looked at him with pleading eyes. "Take me somewhere really fun tonight."

Nodding, he said, "Okay."

CHAPTER 18

Hearing her cell phone ring the second she stepped back into the house, Sarah answered it. With a look of relief, she hung up and gave her sisters an update on Ms. Cecilia's condition.

"Detective Murray just called. He said that Ms. Cecilia's doctors were able to get her stable and that they think she'll make it. She was lucky the bullet didn't hit any major organs."

"Oh, thank God! That's definitely some good news!" Melissa let out a big sigh.

Wanting to be happy for Ms. Cecilia but unable to get her mind off the way her aunt had looked, Jessica simply smiled. Her heart had broken at just the sight of her aunt's neck. That someone could be so malicious to do that on purpose tortured her heart. She needed to find a way to cope.

Pulling him up to the solitude of the guest bedroom, she said, "Nick, do you know of any good nightclubs around here?" She kept him close to her.

"Let me think ... Um, yeah. There's one called Club Paradise. Why?"

"Have you ever seen the movie *Dirty Dancing*?"

"Yes."

"Well, that's my favorite movie, and I want to lose myself dancing like that with you." She let his brown eyes pull her in again. "I want to feel your hands all over my body as we get lost in the music."

"Oh."

"Are you up for that?" Her eyes pleaded with him to say yes.

"Jessica, I'm up for whatever you want to do."

Pulling him into a kiss by his shirt, she did her best to keep her composure. Unfortunately, a couple of tears escaped.

Feeling her need for closeness, when she released her lips from his, he pulled her into his arms and let her cry.

"Did you want to see if your sisters wanted to come too or did you just want it to be the two of us?" he asked once her crying had let up.

"I don't mind if they come. Once we all start dancing, it won't make a difference. I just want to feel your body against mine."

Smiling, he said, "Then we'll do all the sultry dancing you want."

"Hmm, sounds good to me."

She wondered how hot it would get between them.

Letting her sisters know about her and Nick's plan to go to a nightclub, Jessica asked if they wanted to tag along. At first, Sarah questioned if it was the appropriate timing, but when she saw Jessica's disposition show that it was her coping mechanism, she readily accepted the invitation. As for Melissa, since she didn't want to be left at the house by herself, it was an easy yes from her.

Excited to venture out and see more of the Bay Area's nightlife, Jessica anxiously waited to get dressed for going to a nightclub.

With Sarah resuming her responsibility of arranging their aunt's funeral service, she called the funeral home that had taken care of their uncle George to see about transporting her aunt's body into their care.

Meanwhile, Melissa wondered whether or not their aunt even had a will drawn up or if they would just have to plan everything from their memories of her. For a brief moment, she thought about calling their father, but then wondered if he would even know. Realizing that she and her sisters were having to figure it out as they went, she decided to search her aunt's office for a will.

Knowing that she had plenty of time before nightfall, she put her hand on the doorknob and attempted to turn it. Discovering it was locked, Melissa shook her head. She had forgotten that her aunt had always been careful about who saw her private business.

Realizing that either she'd need a key or have to break open the door, Melissa opted for trying to find the key. *But where would she have hidden it?*

Looking at the lock, she tried to think back to the last time she was at the house when Aunt May was still alive. *Did she ever let me know where it was without my realizing it?* Finally, it dawned on her. She needed to check her jewelry box.

Hurrying upstairs, Melissa went over to her aunt's jewelry box on her vanity. Rummaging through the jewelry, she eventually found it, a key slid onto a necklace for safekeeping. With excitement, she hurried back down to the lock and tried it. Sure enough, it was a perfect fit. Happy with her successful sleuthing, she opened the door to see her aunt's preference for organization.

That was when Melissa realized that her aunt must've had a few secrets she wouldn't even tell her nieces; otherwise, why would she need to keep her office door locked?

CHAPTER 19

Beginning her hunt for her aunt's will, Melissa opened the desk's drawers and sifted through papers. Drawer after drawer, there was nothing.

Why did she feel the need to hide her will?

Melissa was turning her aunt's organized office into total chaos. Finding nothing that told her of what her aunt wanted to leave other family members, Melissa was about to give up. It wasn't until she hit a drawer just right that she heard the sound of something drop into the drawer below it. Curious, she removed the drawer to find another key.

Feeling like she was now on a treasure hunt, she wondered what it could possibly be to. Looking around the room, she didn't see a safe or anything else that would require a key to open it. All she saw were pictures of her aunt and uncle with people she didn't recognize and memories of her and her sisters as kids, playing in the yard or goofing off in the house. There were even a few of their aunt with her mom.

Realizing the treasure hunt was now a bust, Melissa decided to end her search for the mysterious treasure. Doing her best to return the office to how it first looked, she carefully reorganized the desk. But as she moved the office chair back into place, one of the wheels caught on the rug underneath it. In her attempt to free the wheel from the snag, she found a floor safe with an entry for a key. "The key!"

Eagerly inserting it into the lock, Melissa released the door and found a large box. Taking it out and setting it on the floor, she opened it to see her aunt's last will and testament. Recognizing that this meant that she and her sisters now had their aunt's own wishes to plan her funeral service, Melissa put the lid back on the box and feverishly looked for Sarah.

"Uncle Gino, why the hell did you shoot my wife?" Damon demanded an answer as they watched the house from his uncle's white '95 Oldsmobile. "That was never part of the plan!"

"Because your wife was going to stab us in the back."

"You don't know that!"

"Damon, why would she head back to the Willards' when she told Detective Murray that she would be staying with her sister?"

"I don't know. Maybe she forgot something."

"Boy, use your head. She was going to look for May Willard's will."

"But why would she do that when the sisters were clearly home?"

"My guess is that she probably didn't know they were home. After all, they only have the detective's nephew's car to use, and it wasn't there, so ..."

"But the Willards' bedroom light was on."

"Damon, people will leave on a light simply to make it look like someone's home. Face it—your wife was trying to screw us over."

"But you could've killed her, damn it!"

"Relax. I'm sure she'll be fine."

"If she dies, her blood is on your hands."

"So be it. But I will not have your wife screwing me out of the fortune the Willards have hidden somewhere." He clenched a fist. "I knew George too long to let his wife's death leave me with nothing!"

"Well, maybe we're still fine. Maybe his nieces still don't have a clue about it or its whereabouts."

"I don't like maybes, Damon. We need to know for certain."

"And how are we supposed to do that?"

"You're going to track them."

"Excuse me?"

"You're going to follow Detective Murray's nephew the next time he takes the girls somewhere."

"And how will that solve our problem if the will is in the house somewhere?"

"By introducing yourself to them in public. They don't know who you are, much less that you're married to their aunt's maid."

Shaking his head, Damon said, "I can't believe that I'm even agreeing to this."

"Damon, all I'm asking you to do is tail the nephew and then make nice with the sisters." He turned the car's engine on to end the stakeout. "I'll drop you off at your car and then you can come back here and follow them to wherever they're going next." He tried to make it look as if he belonged in the neighborhood. "Better yet, get Kyle to come with you. That way, it won't look odd that you're alone."

CHAPTER 20

"Sarah, look what I found!" Melissa found her in the kitchen. "It's Aunt May's will." She put the box on the table.

Pushing her snack to the side, Sarah started to lift the lid on the box when her cell phone rang. "Hello, this is Sarah Parker."

"Ms. Parker, it's Detective Murray. The hospital just called me. Your aunt's maid didn't make it through surgery. Apparently, she lost too much blood."

She felt her heart drop. "Thank you for letting me know." Hanging up, she took a deep breath and told Melissa. "Now Ms. Cecilia's been murdered. Are we going to be next?"

Forgoing looking at the will, Sarah pushed it to the side. Even though she and her sisters hadn't been close to Ms. Cecilia as their aunt had, they still felt saddened by the loss.

"This trip to California is turning into a nightmare!" Sarah buried her face in her hands.

"Who should tell Jessica?" Melissa asked.

"Ugh! I don't know."

"Should we cancel tonight?"

"Honestly, no. I think we could all use the breather. After all, we just get to hear the news of her death; her family will have to handle all the rest."

Nodding, Melissa headed upstairs to give Jessica and Nick the latest update of the week. When she knocked on the doorframe to make her presence known, she suddenly felt like a third wheel when she saw Nick with his hands in Jessica's back pockets.

"Uh, sorry to interrupt, but I've got some more bad news." Melissa looked away to give them privacy.

Swiftly removing his hands, Nick put them around Jessica's waist once she had turned around to face her sister.

"What's wrong now, Melissa?"

"Detective Murray just called. Ms. Cecilia didn't make it."

Immediately grabbing Nick's hands, Jessica didn't know how much more bad news she could take. Had it not been for Nick holding her, she would've collapsed in his arms.

"And you and Sarah have absolutely no idea who shot her?" Jessica asked, looking at Melissa for renewed hope.

"Nope. The gunshot came out of nowhere, and I at least didn't see the shooter. As for Sarah, I don't believe she did either."

"Jessica, with Ms. Cecilia's death, should we cancel going out to the club tonight?" Melissa asked.

Thinking about it for a moment, while also realizing that Ms. Cecilia was more family to their aunt than to them, she decided that going to the nightclub was something they all desperately needed.

"No, I think the club will be helpful. There's only so much tragedy a person can take."

Nodding her understanding, Melissa headed back downstairs.

"Maybe I should add getting drunk to tonight's festivities." Jessica turned back to face Nick.

"No, drinking won't erase their deaths; you'll just end up with a nasty hangover."

"Or it'll make me lose all of my inhibitions and you can drive my body crazy with your mouth." She slipped her hands into his back pockets this time. She could only imagine how he would drive her crazy once they moved beyond just making out.

"Jessica, no. Sex won't relieve your pain either. Because the second we're done, you'll remember that your aunt and her maid are still dead." He removed her hands from his pockets.

"Damn it, I hate that you're right!" She rested her head on his right shoulder.

"I know. And I'm sorry." He tightened his embrace around her.

Getting dressed for the club, the sisters tried to mask the deaths with a brave facade. Going to a nightclub should've been a way for them to relieve some stress and give their emotions a break; instead, it felt like a forced event that caused them to steel themselves.

Jessica even tried thinking about Nick getting to see her in something sexy, but even that couldn't lift her mood. She didn't know what to do. She knew she didn't just want to sit at the house wallowing in her pain, so going out was her only option. She just desperately hoped that Nick could lift her spirits once they were out on that dance floor.

As Melissa searched through her clothes for something club-worthy to wear, she remembered that they still needed to read their aunt May's will. What was so important about it that her aunt had felt the need to keep it hidden in a floor safe? What secrets were she and her sisters about to uncover when they finally read what Aunt May had bequeathed to those she loved?

Looking at the clothes she had brought for the duration of their trip, Sarah didn't see anything that appealed to her enough to want to wear it to the club. Had it not been for the desperate plea in Jessica's eyes, she would've nixed the idea right on the spot. But now, for the sake of her sister, she had to figure out an outfit.

CHAPTER 21

Deciding on a black spaghetti-strap dress that showed off her legs, Jessica matched it with a pair of three-inch black strapped heels. Putting her hair up in a neat bun, she was ready to go. After selecting a purse, she went to see if Melissa and Sarah were ready.

Knocking on Melissa's door, Jessica opened it to see Melissa looking at her choice in a mirror. Pairing a white camisole with a pink skirt with its front pockets outlined in white, she'd completed the look with her own white thee-inch heels and a white headband.

"I wonder what Sarah picked out." Jessica put her head on her sister's shoulder.

"Don't know, but I bet it took her a while to figure it out," Melissa replied.

Even with both dressed up, their mindsets couldn't match their evening wear.

Getting a purse for her stuff, Melissa followed Jessica to their aunt and uncle's bedroom. With the door already open, they found their sister finishing with her shoes.

Settling on a Victoria's Secret black lacy blouse that mirrored a corset, she had slipped on a pair of dark blue jeans and black boots. Leaving her hair down, she was ready to go.

Heading downstairs with her sisters, Jessica called Nick to let him know that they were ready. Now just wanting to get the night over with, Sarah thought about telling Jessica and Melissa to go without her. Unfortunately, it wasn't but ten minutes later when they heard the familiar sound of Nick's convertible pulling into the driveway. *I guess there's no backing out now.*

Turning off the engine, Nick got out of his convertible and knocked on the door.

Opening the door for him, Jessica showed off her black dress as she took in his navy blue polo shirt, jeans, and Doc Martens.

Smiling, he said, "You look hot!" He took in the dress that accentuated her figure. She couldn't have looked sexier to him.

"Thanks." She shyly smiled.

"You're welcome. Are you and your sisters ready to go?" His eyes shifted to them.

They gave him uneasy smiles for having to witness the interaction.

"Okay. Then let's go." He held the door open for them to head out to his car. Briefly stopping Jessica with an arm around her waist, he whispered to her. "You should know that you're already making this hard on me."

"You have yet to see me dancing."

"If only your sisters weren't waiting to get into my car." He let her go.

Getting back into the car, Nick felt like it was a dressed-up version of the drive to see the sisters' aunt. Even with the comfort that came from holding Jessica's hand, the tone in the car pleaded for him to turn on the radio—anything but the silence that the sisters were putting him through.

Arriving at Club Paradise, Nick easily found a parking spot. After he let the girls out, the four made their way to the entrance. They walked up to a man dressed in a classic tuxedo; standing underneath a plum-colored awning, he guarded the entrance to the club.

"ID, please."

Taking out their wallets one by one, the sisters and Nick proved their eligibility for the club. Satisfied, he moved aside to allow them entry. With Nick holding the door open for them, the sisters headed inside for what they hoped would turn into a fun night out.

Upon entering the club, they were greeted with pictures of the club's staff, with various bands that had performed there, on the walls. Seeing the memories made Melissa remember her aunt's office and the pictures she'd proudly displayed.

When they had reached the end of the hall, a velvet curtain halted them. Finding the opening, they were provided with stairs leading to the dance floor, tables, and bar.

The club was packed. Besides the filled dance floor, the bartenders were overwhelmed with customers, and the majority of the tables were filled with club-goers enjoying conversation.

"I guess we weren't the only ones with this idea," Nick stated. He wondered if the sisters would just want to turn around and leave.

With determination, Jessica took his hand. "I don't care. I need this!" She led him down the stairs, Melissa and Sarah following.

Straightaway, they claimed one of the tables.

"Do we want to get drinks first or go to the dance floor?" Nick asked.

"Dance," Jessica easily decided, dropping her purse on the table.

Once again, she led him to her destination, leaving Melissa and Sarah at the table while she let loose with Nick.

Finding a place just for themselves, Jessica let go and let Nick see her moves. Dancing so close to him, she easily found herself in the zone. As the song led their moves, she felt his hands keep his body against hers. The feeling was just what she wanted. He made her feel sexy while also giving her a reason to forget about her aunt and the maid.

CHAPTER 22

Opening the curtain, Damon watched the sisters and Nick grab a table before he and Jessica left for the dance floor. "There they are, Kyle."

Watching the two enjoy being so close to each other, Damon began to wonder if there was something going on between them. Since Cecilia hadn't let him in on any details prior to her sudden death, he couldn't help but wonder if Jessica Parker and the detective's nephew had taken a romantic interest in each other. If they had, he just might be able to work that to his advantage. After all, the girl's guard might be down whenever she was around him.

Continuing down the stairs with his younger brother tagging along, Damon went to go find out.

"You were definitely right about your moves." Nick grinned, taking her into his arms when a slow song came on.

"You certainly know what you're doing as well." She kissed him.

"I've just got a good dance partner." He was enjoying keeping her close to him.

Smiling, Jessica stared back into his eyes. Being this close was easy with him. It seemed like everything they did together felt so natural, so right. *This must've been how Aunt May felt with Uncle George.* Her only worry was if she was just feeling this way because they were still in the honeymoon phase of their relationship.

But was it just that? She had been in other relationships before, and it had never felt this easy—at least not at first. Sure, the newness of the relationship would bring its usual butterflies and awkwardness, but it never felt like this for her. There was just something about being in Nick's arms, whether for affection or dancing, that just made her not want to leave them. Maybe she had experienced love at first sight with him. Maybe she was in love with Nick Powell even though they'd only known each other for a few days.

Whispering in his ear, she said, "Nick, I think I may be in love with you." Her eyes shined with adoration for him when she looked into his.

"And you don't think that's too fast for you?" He was partly teasing, partly curious.

"I think I'm experiencing an easiness with you I've never felt before. It's not just the comfort of your arms but also the simplicity of how we are together. Yes, this is new, but it's not awkward and it's not work. It feels completely natural." Her expression hoped he understood.

"Then I'm in love with you too." He kissed her.

Though deeply sensual, this kiss was different from their other passionate ones. It expressed to her not only his desire for her, but showed her how much he truly cared. He took his time with it and let her experience every sensation his lips brought to her mouth. The kiss told her he felt the same way.

When they released, they felt a shift in how they saw each other. The sensuousness of their intimacy had seared an imprint on their relationship. A kiss that perfectly explained how each felt now permanently bonded them together.

"Nick ..." Her mind felt blown by it, and her heart now knew that it belonged to him.

"I know."

Feeling the tenderness of the kiss mark a permanent memory in his mind, Nick now knew that he would be asking Jessica to marry him once he could get his grandmother's ring. He had never experienced something so sensuous before. The kiss perfectly illustrated how well he and Jessica fit together and were each other's perfect complement.

Watching her sister and Nick dance so sensually together and share a sensuous kiss as if they were the only two on the dance floor, Melissa found herself suddenly wishing she weren't single. The way they enjoyed each other as the music propelled their movements made her crave that same touch.

Her most recent ex, Cody Fischer, had been the relationship she thought was going to turn into "'the one." But instead of proposing when they reached their five-year anniversary, he had told her that he had decided he wanted to travel the world—without her. It had been such a heart-crushing moment when she realized that he was more excited to travel the continents than have a future with her.

As she longingly watched her sister publicly show her affection for Nick, two men approached the table.

"Hi, I'm Damon Riley, and this is my brother, Kyle." He'd found a way to meet them.

"Uh, hi. I'm Melissa and this is my sister Sarah."

"Are you ladies alone or waiting on dates?"

"Actually, we're with my sister and her ... boyfriend."

"Oh. Well, in that case, would both of you like to dance?"

"Um, that's okay. It's been a long day, and we're both tired." Melissa immediately felt uneasy about him.

Unsure of what to do to accomplish his uncle's goal, he looked to his brother for help.

Following his eyes, Melissa found Kyle's hazel eyes alluring. Something about his reserved nature made her curious about him.

"If you're not interested in dancing with him, you can certainly dance with me instead." Kyle took in her light green eyes and immediately felt a connection.

Giving him a sweet smile, she had no problem getting up from her seat and following him out onto the dance floor.

"Now, how about you?" Damon turned his attention to Sarah.

"No, thanks. Someone's got to watch their purses."

Her look of disinterest told him that there was no way she was saying yes to him.

Accepting her rejection, Damon went to the bar. Even though he was successful in using his brother as a means of getting close to the Parker sisters, it had burned him that he had been told no.

Following Kyle out onto the dance floor, Melissa felt their natural chemistry at just the touch of his hand. As the sparks let her know that she held a deeper interest in him, she wondered if he felt the same. As they danced together, the music determining their pace, she watched him do his best to maintain a respectful distance between them while also purposefully remaining in somewhat close proximity to her.

However, it was when the music had once again returned to a slower beat that she had her answer. As their positioning changed and Melissa welcomed his arms around her, his eyes told her that he was very much into her. When he spoke, she leaned in so she could hear him better. "I'd ask if you wanted to find a table for two once the dancing's over, but I'm thinking it would be a little too soon for that."

Hearing his question reveal his courteous nature, Melissa found herself surprised. Not only did the two have a mutual interest for each other, but he knew how to charm her as well.

CHAPTER 23

"We'll have to make sure to exchange numbers before we leave," Melissa said.

"I'd like that. But just so you know, I'll be heading back to New York City at the end of the week."

Her eyes lit up. "You will?"

"Yeah. I've got an internship at a law firm starting next week."

"Then we at least won't have to worry about any long-distance issues; my sisters and I live in New York City."

He smiled. "It sounds like I'm in need of a tour guide, then."

Returning the smile she said, "I would love to give you a personal tour of the city."

"Then we will definitely have to exchange numbers." He adjusted his arms around her to bring her closer to him.

Returning to the table, Jessica and Nick took a break from dancing. "Who's Melissa dancing with?" Jessica asked.

Putting an arm around Jessica's chair, Nick felt the responsibility of an older brother as he checked out Melissa's new guy.

"His name's Kyle Riley. He and his brother came over to our table while you two were dancing. His brother, Damon, asked if we wanted to dance, and Melissa chose Kyle."

"Ouch! Sounds like it sucks to be his brother," Nick replied.

"I guess. I just knew I had no interest in dancing with either brother." Sarah shrugged. "Tonight was for Jessica."

"Thanks, Sarah, and believe me, I needed it." Jessica looked at Nick.

Saving the PDA for later, he winked at her. "I'm going to go get us some drinks. You want anything, Sarah?"

"A water's fine."

He nodded. "I'll be right back." He fought the urge to kiss Jessica in order not to make Sarah feel uncomfortable.

Watching Nick heading toward him, Damon wondered if he should strike up a conversation with him. After all, Nick didn't know that he was Kyle's brother. To him, Damon was just another patron enjoying his drink at the bar. Hoping he could get Nick to give him information, Damon figured it was worth a shot. "Just to let you know, the wait for a drink's a bit long."

"Thanks."

Nick watched the bartenders, hoping one would free up soon.

"Met any hot girls yet?"

"Actually, I've already got a girl I'm seeing."

"Does she have any sisters?"

"Two, but I don't know that they're looking." Nick watched a bartender finish making a drink and hoped he would be next.

"Oh. Well, I understand. Come to think about it, I probably shouldn't even be here right now. I just lost my wife and was looking to numb the pain somehow."

"I'm sorry. That sucks."

Nick let the bartender know what he wanted.

"Yeah, that girl was the love of my life," Damon pressed.

He had hoped Cecilia's death could benefit him, but so far, Nick wasn't biting.

Watching the bartender make each drink, Nick anxiously waited for them to be ready. "Well, I'm sorry about your wife."

Damon watched Nick walk back to the table.

Damn it! Maybe Kyle will be able to get something out of Melissa. He looked over at the dance floor and watched them continue dancing together.

CHAPTER 24

"Are you ready to head back to the table?" Melissa asked Kyle as she felt her energy for dancing wind down.

"Sure, we can head back."

He was glad his uncle Gino had urged him to tag along with his older brother. He didn't know why Damon had been so insistent on them meeting up with the table of four when he had never met them before, but he was happy he had.

Grabbing an available seat from another table, Sarah became the fifth wheel. But as the conversation flowed and Kyle got drinks for him and Melissa, Sarah didn't mind it. She was just happy to see both of her sisters enjoying their night out.

Meanwhile, Damon cringed as he watched his brother easily prove his pairing up with Melissa as fate. Being on the outside and looking in, Damon drowned his annoyance in his drink. He wasn't considered an ugly guy. In fact, with short dirty-blond hair and light blue eyes, he had managed to catch Cecilia's attention easily.

This better work! He finished his drink and left the club to wait for his brother in his car.

"I'm so glad Melissa met Kyle tonight. Now we'll get to double date with them!" Jessica led Nick back into the guest room.

"Have you been anxious to do that?" He closed the door behind him.

"Sometimes." She sat down and took off her shoes. "Will you unzip me, please?"

Sliding the zipper down, he took in her bare skin. Wearing a dress that didn't require a bra pushed his imagination into wondering what her bare breasts looked like. He wanted to kiss her neck and explore her skin with his hands.

"Thanks." Briefly smiling, she turned her head to look at him. Walking over to the dresser, she took out her pajama pants and a nightshirt.

He'd never seen a woman look so sexy. Just watching her slip off the dress, put on what she wore to bed, and then let her hair down, he had no words.

Can I really just go to sleep next to her now that I've seen her this way? The thought crept into his mind. Just the knowledge that she wouldn't have a bra on if he slipped a hand under her shirt and slid it up her body made him wonder if he was strong enough not to give in to the temptation. Despite the fact that he now had a new belief in God, he didn't know if waiting for marriage needed to be just as important.

Jessica broke into his thoughts. "Are you going to bed like that, Nick?"

He had yet to take his shoes off since they had come into the room.

"Funny, but I was just thinking."

"About what?"

"Just sleeping in the bed with you." He decided to just be blunt about it and not sift through his thoughts.

"Ah, so we're back to the topic of sex again." She took a seat on the bed.

"Jessica, you make me want you. But I want to do this the right way."

"Which means getting married first so we can finally give in to our desire for each other?"

"That is what I'm struggling with."

"How so?"

"Well, you know that I believe in God, but I guess I'm still struggling with the rest of it."

"Nick, if you want to wait for marriage, we can. After that kiss tonight, I'm yours. Now and forever."

"So you think we'll be able to just sleep next to each other and that's it?" His doubt clearly showed all over his face.

"I'm not saying it won't be tempting to explore that desire some, but I also think I would miss your presence if you weren't right next to me."

As if it were so normal for her, she reached her fingers up to the nape of his neck and began running her fingers through his hair.

"I can definitely get used to this." He gave her a kiss on the cheek.

"Then why don't you get ready for bed and then we can just go to sleep?" She smiled.

"I'd like that." He took off his shoes and jeans.

Climbing under the covers with her, he kept their close proximity with her in his arms. As he held her against him, the knowledge that she was braless didn't matter anymore. He was content with just holding her close to him. It was an experience and a feeling that he hadn't known before but somehow felt so comfortable with.

Maybe it was God pressing the contentedness on his heart. Maybe he was starting to understand why God intended sex to be a sacred act, an act so intimate that it was meant to be shared only between a husband and his wife. All he knew for sure right now was that he loved Jessica. His feelings for her grew with every day they saw each other.

"I am pretty comfortable with you like this," Jessica added to his thoughts.

He kissed her neck. "Marry me, Jessica." The words just came out, but his heart meant them.

She turned around to face him. "What?"

"Marry me. I love you, and I want to marry you. I was going to ask you in a more thought out way later on, but right now, it just feels right. Right now, with you in my arms like this, I can't help but want to ask you."

"I thought you were going to wait until you had your grandmother's ring first." She returned her fingers to the nape of his neck.

"I can still do that if you want."

"Nick, waiting for the ring honestly doesn't matter to me. I love you, and I want to spend my life loving you." She smiled, giving him a kiss.

"No waiting until the dust settles to really figure out if what you feel for me is the result of this week and not your true feelings?" He looked at her with curious eyes.

"Nope," she easily answered. "Having you here with me has been a godsend. Without your companionship, Nick, I have no idea how I would've gotten through everything that's happened since finding out my aunt had been murdered."

"Huh, so I've just been a distraction for you?" he teased.

"Funny, but you know it's a lot more than that." She gave him a look that said she was not impressed.

"I know." He ran a hand through her hair. "And I know that you still have yet to answer my question."

She took a moment to think about how she finally wanted to answer him. "Yes." She gave him a big smile. "Yes, I'll marry you."

Watching his eyes widen with surprise, she laughed.

"I love you, Jessica Parker." He pulled her onto him in his excitement.

"I love you too, Nick Powell." She laughed again.

Realizing that she could feel his member more prominently now that she was lying on top of him, she sat up to straddle him. She began to take her shirt off, but he stopped her.

"Jessica, not yet. Let's wait until we've made our life together official."

Dropping her shirt, she leaned down to kiss him, letting him know she understood.

As she returned to the comfort of his arms, he held her close to him as they both drifted off to sleep.

Jessica wasn't just in love; she had met the man she had been made for. He embodied all the qualities she not only needed in a partner but also abundantly showed her the qualities she didn't even know she desired.

CHAPTER 25

Waking up to being held in his arms, Jessica enjoyed the quiet. Just feeling him against her made her soak in her time with him.

As she felt Nick wake up, she realized that she wished she was already married to him. She loved being held by him and the ease of intimacy their time together brought them.

"Morning, Nick." She bit her lip from nervousness. She was now his fiancée, even if she didn't have a physical ring to prove it.

"Morning, Jess." He couldn't help but kiss her. "I'm liking this already." She looked so beautiful to him.

She smiled. "Me too. It's too bad we're not already married or I could give you morning sex."

"Soon enough, Jess." He slipped a hand through her bed head and took in her beauty.

This moment wasn't about sex to him. It was about his really seeing her for the beautiful woman she was. Just the way her sleepiness gave a raw perfection to her made him think he was the luckiest man alive. He was going to get to put a ring on her finger and call her his wife. He couldn't have been more blessed.

As she stared back into his eyes, Jessica enjoyed the way his hair had become messed up from his sleep. It brought a pureness to him and reminded her that no man is perfect.

"I guess I need to tell your uncle thank you for calling my sister and telling her that we needed to come to California. Had she not, I would've never met you."

"I owe him a big thank-you myself for asking me to help him."

All she could do was give him a big smile in return. She had never been so happy before, so content with life. She glanced over at the door, wondering what her sisters would think if after briefly knocking, they opened it and caught them in bed together. Since they both still had their clothes on, it wouldn't be as awkward.

He saw her brief glance at the door. "Are you worried about your sisters seeing us together like this?"

"The thought had crossed my mind." She shrugged.

"Should we get up, then?"

She groaned. "I don't want to. I don't want to leave the warmth of your arms." She nuzzled herself against him.

Smiling, he slipped a hand under her shirt and caressed her back. "This does feel pretty perfect."

Giving him a kiss, she stopped his caressing and took off his shirt. Laying her head on his chest, she rested her hand over his heart. "I like being this close to you."

Nick couldn't help but smile. Seeing that she was content with just her head on his chest, without it being the result of sex, made him feel so happy. She wasn't trying to turn him on; she simply desired the intimacy this closeness gave them.

"When do you want to tell your sisters about our getting engaged?" He intertwined their fingers.

"When we go downstairs for breakfast."

"Did you want me to get down on one knee first since you don't have a ring to show them?" He wrapped his other arm around her.

"You don't have to." She looked up at him.

"That's not what I asked."

"Then yes. We can tell them that we've talked about it and that when you get your grandmother's ring, you'll make it official."

"I'm fine with that."

He pulled her into a quick kiss before they both got out of bed.

Realizing she needed to take a shower before getting dressed, she paused to see if he wanted to join her or head home instead.

"Nick?"

"Yeah?"

"Do you remember what I said before about taking a shower with you?"

"Yep."

"Well, did you want to join me or head home for it instead? It's not about having sex; I just want to keep this closeness going."

He closed the gap between them. "I would love to take a shower with you, but I don't think it's a good idea, at least not yet."

"Oh."

"Jess, if I took a shower with you, we would likely end up having sex. There's no way I wouldn't desire you once I saw you naked and wet."

"You do have a point." She realized that it would be the same for her. She couldn't help but look at him with disappointment in her eyes.

He smiled at her desire. "Jess, it won't be long until you're Mrs. Nicholas Powell."

Giving him a kiss for the reminder, Jessica grabbed what she needed for her shower and left Nick to get redressed before he headed home.

Stepping into the shower, Jessica felt the water cleanse her body. She couldn't help but imagine Nick joining her. Even though she knew he was right to hold off on taking a shower together, just the idea of them together like that wouldn't leave her thoughts.

But as she thought about them waiting for marriage, the significance of his choosing for them to do that rocked her. He wasn't only placing an extreme amount of importance on sex itself; he was also showing her how important sex with her was to him.

Nick clearly cared deeply about her and was constantly showing her that. She couldn't wait to be that close to him, to experience his love for her without words. To think that when they finally did have sex, they would be husband and wife amazed her just the same. She had never placed the same importance on waiting for marriage, but with Nick's belief in God, his view on it was changing her own.

CHAPTER 26

As she rinsed off the last of her body wash, turning off the water before stepping out of the shower and grabbing a towel, Jessica found herself glad that Nick had insisted they didn't share the shower.

It had given her time to think. Her parents had never instilled in her, or her sisters, the value of waiting for marriage. As far as she knew, they hadn't waited themselves, and the topic itself was just never discussed. Fortunately for her, she had never been one to fall to peer pressure or feel the need to rid herself of the virginity label by a specific age.

Looking in the mirror, with her towel wrapped around her, Jessica found herself imagining Nick in the shower as the water drenched his body. Just the way his muscles would look when he cleared it from his face kept her thinking about how hot he was. She could picture the heat between them rising if he had walked into the bathroom and saw her with her freshly showered skin. It would be damn hard for them to stay virgins at that point.

Shaking herself out of her thoughts, she finished in the bathroom before heading back into the guest bedroom to get dressed. Hearing his convertible pull into the driveway, she smiled with excitement. He was back. Hurrying down the stairs to greet him, she felt as if she were back in high school.

It wasn't until she opened the front door and watched him get out, seeing his freshly showered look that made him seem so much hotter, that she knew why she had desired him so much.

"Hey." He met her at the door. Pulling her to him, he gave her a kiss. His voice even sounded sexier.

Breathing in his cologne, she said, "Nick, I'm ovulating right now."

"Oh."

"I'm just telling you because I think it's the reason I've desired you so much."

"Ah."

"Yep. So once this week is over, my desire for you will still be there; it just won't be as heightened."

"Is that your way of assuring me you'll still love me?" he teased.

"Nick ..."

"Jess, regardless of the reason, I know what's between us is real."

Wrapping her arms around his neck, she said, "I guess it's a good thing that we never had sex because I could pretty much guarantee you that your life would be changing in about nine months."

He returned the gesture with his arms around her waist. "Jessica, if we had, I'd be okay with it. I'm in love with you. That's why I asked you to marry me. I just want to be with you."

Smiling, she enjoyed the heightened sensitivity that made her notice everything about him that made him a man. It was also nice not having that pressure of sex to go along with it but instead just enjoying how attracted she was to him and him to her.

"By the way, you smell really good."

"You like my cologne?"

"Yeah, I do."

"I guess I'll have to make sure I wear it on a regular basis from now on, then." He grinned. "Or at least once we're married and I know you're ovulating." He lowered his voice for impact.

Shaking her head at him, she ran her fingers through the hair at the nape of his neck. "You'd better not use what I told you against me!"

"And not take advantage of the extra sex you'll want to have during that time of the month?" He raised his eyebrows. "Your heightened desire benefits me too."

She gave him a kiss. "Then we'd better go tell my sisters about our unofficial engagement."

Walking into the kitchen together, they found her sisters already eating breakfast.

"Morning, you two. That was some night last night," Melissa said by way of greeting them.

"It sure was. Have you called Kyle yet?" Jessica asked, Nick staying behind her for support.

"Yeah, we ended up texting before I went to sleep. He wants to take all of us out on his uncle's yacht tomorrow."

"Really?" Sarah asked.

"Yep. I got the feeling that he really wanted to just invite me but then thought I would feel too uncomfortable since we're still just getting to know each other."

"Sounds like he really cares for you, Melissa." Sarah found herself impressed by Kyle's level of consideration.

"Yeah, I think he does. I felt the same kind of attraction Jessica and Nick felt for each other the first time they met." Melissa glanced at each.

Looking at each other, they thought back to that day. The love they had for each other began the moment they met.

"Sarah, will you be okay being the fifth wheel again?" Melissa remembered how she'd dealt with it last night.

"Of course I'll be fine. As long as my sisters are both happy, I'm totally good by myself."

"Speaking of, we've got something to tell you both." Jessica took a deep breath. As she looked at Nick, he nodded. "We've decided that we want to get married." Jessica looked at her sisters for their responses.

Melissa easily gave her acceptance. "I figured as much."

"Sarah, what do you think?" Jessica asked.

"I think that Nick makes you happy. I see it in your eyes whenever you look at him."

"He does." Jessica looked at him with a smile.

"When were you thinking about getting married?" Sarah asked.

"Probably when everything's settled down with your aunt's murder investigation," Nick answered.

"We just decided on it this morning. But it won't be official until he gives me his grandmother's ring," Jessica added.

"I can appreciate that." Melissa looked at her bare ring finger.

"Once it is, how much planning will be involved?" Sarah asked, already mentally preparing a list.

"Not much. I'm just thinking of having a justice of the peace doing the honors," Jessica answered. "Since neither of us have big families, I think just having those most important to us there will be fine."

"That certainly makes planning easier," Sarah agreed. "And right now I like simple."

"Does this mean you plan on staying here in California, Jessica?" Sarah asked.

"Yeah, it does," she answered with a bittersweet expression. She felt Nick wrap his arms around her for added support.

"We've got my house to live in until we find a house to buy," Nick added. He knew this transition would be hard not only on her but on her sisters as well.

"You could always live here. With Aunt May gone and our mom stuck where she is, this house will remain empty once we leave," Sarah offered.

"There is that option." Nick looked at Jessica. He could already see her heart breaking from the reality of this next step in her life.

"Well then, I guess we've got a courthouse wedding to plan," Sarah finally announced.

"Yeah, we do." Jessica's once-cheerful disposition had dramatically changed as she thought about having to say goodbye to her sisters when it was time for them to go back to their apartment.

"Jess, it'll be okay." Nick turned her to face him once her sisters had left the kitchen.

"I know it will. It's just ... this is becoming real and I'm not so sure I'm ready for that. I'm not sure I'm ready to say goodbye to my sisters."

Pulling her to him, Nick let her grieve another loss.

CHAPTER 27

Going shopping for a simple white dress and dresses for her sisters, Jessica and her sisters enjoyed the day as they prepared for the celebration. Finding a sundress that embodied her personality, Jessica imagined saying her vows to Nick in it. With similar white heels to her black ones, all she had left to figure out was her hair and jewelry. Should she wear a veil, to keep with some of the tradition, or leave her face unshielded by a barrier? As for the jewelry, she was sure her aunt would have something she could wear.

After telling his mom about Jessica, Nick was easily granted his grandmother's engagement ring. The ring couldn't have fit Jessica more perfectly. The look told of her free spirit, while the diamond's size embraced her simple nature.

Picking out their wedding bands, with his uncle's help, all Nick had to do now was get a tux. He could've easily been fine with a regular black suit and tie, but he felt the event called for nicer attire.

Returning to their aunt and uncle's house to get ready to become Nick's wife, Jessica took a moment to spend some time with her aunt as she smelled her flowers. Letting their floral scent take her back to when she felt the closest with her aunt, she breathed in the memories. As she embraced the warm sunlight, she could feel her aunt's spirit all around her. Jessica had never felt more at peace. Nick was meant to be hers, and her aunt simply confirmed that.

"Jessica, hurry up. Detective Murray's going to be here soon to take us to the courthouse," Sarah called out to her from the front porch.

"Okay, I'm coming."

Taking a last moment to smell her aunt's favorite flower, Jessica headed back inside. Slipping on her dress that resembled Sandy's from the movie *Grease*, she put on her heels. Letting her sisters do her hair and makeup, she watched her bridal look come together. The only thing missing was her aunt's jewelry. Once they were finished, she would search through her aunt's jewelry box for the perfect earrings and necklace to wear.

Standing in front of the mirror, looking at the complete picture, Jessica wished both her mom and aunt could've been there. Doing her best not to cry for their missing presence, she put her mindset on looking forward to officially becoming Nick's wife.

"Are you ready to go?" Sarah asked her with an arm around her as she and Melissa joined her in looking in the mirror. "Detective Murray's here."

"Yeah, I am." She took a moment to revel in their bond. "I love you both so much."

"We know." Melissa hugged her.

Joining her sisters, Jessica headed downstairs to see the detective waiting for them in his usual suit and tie.

"Nick's already at the courthouse with his mom," Detective Murray informed them.

Nodding, the girls followed him out to his car. Fastening her seat belt, Jessica looked down at her left hand and imagined it with both an engagement and wedding ring on it. The thought jolted her heart. She was ready to say "I do" to him and accept the wedding ring he would soon slide on her finger.

Arriving at the courthouse minutes later, Jessica and her sisters followed the detective inside. The second she saw Nick in his tux, Jessica was hit with the biggest butterflies she had ever felt.

Seeing her walk in, Nick felt as if his heart was bursting with joy. Jessica had never been more radiant, and her smile told him just how excited she was to leave the courthouse as his wife.

"I believe I do have a question to ask you before we start the ceremony," Nick reminded her.

Getting down on one knee, he showed her his grandmother's engagement ring. "Jessica Marie Parker, will you marry me?"

Watching her immediately nod her head yes, he slid his grandmother's engagement ring onto her left ring finger, kissing her. "Now it's time to make it permanent."

Smiling with happiness, Jessica easily took his hand as the two prepared to have their ceremony officiated by the justice of the peace.

With their families watching, Nick and Jessica vowed their hearts to each other. Exchanging wedding rings, they were announced as husband and wife. Taking his cue to kiss her, Nick dipped Jessica back and sealed her new title as his wife.

Being quick to take a picture with her phone, Melissa captured the moment forever.

CHAPTER 28

"Mr. and Mrs. Nick Powell. I really like it!" Jessica looked at Nick as he drove them to his house after the justice of the peace and their families congratulated them.

"Me too." He picked up her hand and kissed it.

She smiled. She had never felt so in love before.

Nick had never been happier. Hearing Jessica vow her love to him for the rest of her life had filled him with so much happiness. And now to get to wake up to her for their rest of their life together, well, he just had no words.

"You ready to have that sleepover in my bed now?" Nick grinned.

"Yes." She looked down at her ring. When she finally had sex with him, it would now be as his wife. The thought completely changed her perspective on being that intimate with him.

"I promise you that it'll be worth the wait." He glanced at her.

"I don't doubt it, Nick. It's just a lot of change to take in.

"I know it is." He slipped his hand into hers. "But I'm right here to take it in with you."

"I love you so much." His hand in hers and his reassuring voice gave her so much comfort.

"I love you so much too, Jess." He pulled into his driveway and parked. Once he turned off the engine, she turned to look at him.

"Thank you for making us wait until this point." Unbuckling her seat belt, she straddled him.

"You're welcome, Jess." He watched her intently. Her movements were calculated as she unbuckled his seat belt.

"I'm ready to be yours now." She unbuckled his belt and opened his pants.

"Do you not want us to wait until we get inside?"

"I just know that I want you." She let his mouth know what her lips wanted.

As if it were déjà vu, he felt her grind against his member. Easily relenting to her seduction, Nick carried her inside. Locking the door to the outside world, he carried her to his bedroom. The second he set her down, his pants fell to his ankles.

"Sorry about that. I guess I was just too eager." She smiled as he bent down to remove his shoes and clear his pants from his legs.

He kissed her. "It's not a problem for me." He helped her remove her sundress, exposing her naked breasts for the first time. "You are so beautiful, Jess!" He returned his lips to hers.

Feeling his passion melt into hers, Jessica took her time taking off his tux. She wanted to enjoy every minute of their foreplay and not rush through it for the sake of finally getting to the sex.

Picking her up, he carried her to his bed, gently laying her down with her heels still fastened to her feet.

"I still need to take off my shoes."

"Let me. I like this view."

Picking up each foot, he unfastened the strap to remove the shoe from it, all the while looking at the beauty that awaited him on his bed.

With her shoes off, he crawled onto the bed, hovering over her. Lowering his mouth to her breasts, he tasted each one. "I knew they would taste good!" Smiling, he briefly looked up at her before returning to enjoy another taste.

As he got to know each breast, teasing her with his tongue, he watched her body arch as she asked for more. Watching her eyes close, he easily obliged. Hearing her moaning from the feel of his mouth against her most sensitive skin, he continued with his tongue.

Feeling the ecstasy he drove through her body, Jessica took hold of his shoulders with a firm grip. She wanted to be closer to him. She wanted to feel him inside her, pushing her to the point of exhaustion and making her forget about the emotional roller coaster she had been on since arriving in California. She was ready for more.

"Nick ..." Her breathing was hard and shallow. "I want you against me. I want to feel your member against me." She pulled his mouth to hers, slipping her fingers in his hair. She wanted to feel how turned on he was for her.

Forgoing more of the deliciousness of her breasts in his mouth, he kissed her with the passion he'd been wanting to release on their first date. Sliding a hand down her back, he slipped it inside her underwear, caressing her butt and causing her to press her pelvis against his. Taking a break from her mouth, he enjoyed her neck. Hearing her moan out her delight, he knew he was getting close.

"Ah ... Nick." Jessica returned the passion he showed her.

"Are you ready?" He could feel his member anxious for the release.

As if words were no longer needed, she moved his hand to her underwear and directed it to take them off. With ease, he slid them down her legs in a way that would make her feel every sensation. In response, she opened her legs to him. She was ready.

"I never bought any protection, Jess."

"I don't care, Nick."

Proving true to her word, she slipped her hands around the rim of his boxers and began sliding them down. "I want you. Now."

Briefly showing her his erection, he returned his mouth to hers. He was ready to make them one. Feeling her legs press against his, he knew she was ready to give him her virginity. He stopped for a moment to whisper into her ear, "I'm going to love your body so hard that you're going to be breathless when I'm done."

Returning to enjoying her kiss, he entered her. He knew she had felt it when he heard the slightest of gasps escape her mouth. Mentally smiling, he brought his thrusts into a rhythm as he took her body through the motions. With every thrust, he could feel her legs keeping tightly against his as their intimacy took them to a sexual bliss with each other.

It was the purest of loves as their closeness took them to an even deeper connection. Knowing that their first time together was as husband and wife hit Nick hard. It made him appreciate the equal love and desire they had for each other even more, and when they finished, it would now be *their* bed they would go to sleep in.

Feeling the friction Nick created with his thrusts, Jessica felt a new sensation surge through her. Grabbing his comforter, she experienced her first orgasm, allowing him to reach his peak and collapse next to her.

CHAPTER 29

Coming down from her orgasm, Jessica wrapped herself in Nick's arms as he lay beside her. "That was amazing!"

"Enjoyed your first time, Mrs. Powell?"

"Yes!" She kissed him. "As torturous as you were to me, it felt exhilarating!"

"It is my goal to satisfy you." He grinned.

"Nick, you did way more than that!" She ran a hand over his chest. "You made me feel sexy when you got me there."

"Jessica, you are sexy." He slid a hand over her leg.

She pulled him into another kiss that caused him to slide back on top of her. "I love you for wanting to be my husband."

"And I love you for accepting my desire for that. Jessica, my heart was yours the moment I met you." He smiled. "Now let's go get something to eat because loving you has made me hungry." After letting her up, they got dressed to go into the kitchen.

"Nick, we'll need to head back to my aunt and uncle's house to get my stuff." Sitting on a barstool, she waited to see what he had for food options.

"We can definitely do that." He went through each cupboard, showing her what he had.

"I'll also need to arrange to have my stuff brought over here from New York."

As she watched him open his home to her, she could feel the soreness from their first time. It also dawned on her that since she had passed on his using protection, she could be pregnant right now.

"We'll get that done too."

Looking around at his decor, she wondered if she could be comfortable there and call it home.

He watched her survey his bachelor pad. He wondered how much of it she was going to want to change. "You like how I decorate?"

"It's fine."

"Jess, it's okay if you don't like some of my stuff."

"Nick, I'm not going to redecorate your house ... if that's what you're worried about. I'll simply just add my stuff to it."

"You say that now." He was trying to tease her, but it wasn't working.

"I'm serious. I have no intention of making you feel like this isn't your home anymore." Her expression proved her words. "Besides, once we start looking for a house, then we'll have our place."

"Jessica, even though my name's on the title, I want you to feel at home here too. After all, the second we said 'I do,' my stuff became yours and yours became mine."

"Maybe symbolically, but realistically, your stuff is still your stuff. Hence the need for our own house."

"Are we actually having our first argument as husband and wife?" Nick chuckled, coming around the counter.

She sighted. "I just want the house I live in to feel like my home. Right now yours doesn't." That was only one of her concerns.

Pulling her into his arms, he asked, "Jess, what's this really about?"

"What do you mean?"

"If this house won't be where you feel most at home, we can always do as Sarah suggested and make your aunt and uncle's house our new home."

She was feeling an overwhelming amount of emotion. "I guess it's all just a lot to process. And since I said I was fine with not using protection, I could be pregnant right now."

Giving her a compassionate smile, he said, "I get it. It is a lot. And if you *are* pregnant after our first time, then we'll get to add the excitement of being parents in nine months to it all."

All Jessica could do right then was cry. Burying her face in the warmth of his neck, she let out the mixture of emotions she felt. She loved that he was so understanding.

"Jessica, I just want you to be happy," he whispered to her, kissing her head.

"I love you so much," she said through tears.

"You already know how I feel," he teased.

Climbing back into his convertible, Nick and Jessica headed to her aunt and uncle's house to pack up her suitcase and bring it back over to his house. It was going to be strange not returning to New York City with her sisters, but she was Nick's wife now, and that meant her city life with her sisters was over.

"Will you want to come back to New York City with me to help me pack up my stuff?" The major change of their last-minute nuptials was now sinking in.

"Sure. I can if you want me to."

She nodded. "I'm going to have to get my last name changed, which means a new driver's license and credit cards."

"You'll have time to do all of that." Nick glanced at her and could see her anxiety building up.

"Of course, I might as well just wait until we move all of my stuff here since I'll have to get a California driver's license." Her mind kept going. "I also need a new Social Security card."

Returning his car to the familiarity of her aunt and uncle's driveway, Nick parked it and killed the engine. "Jessica." He zapped her out of her zone.

"What?"

"We'll make time for you to do all of that. Right now we just need you to get your suitcase packed and ready to take to my house."

Taking a breath, she nodded her head. Unbuckling her seat belt, she was about to open her door when she realized something. "Nick, I forgot to call my sisters to find out if they would even be home."

"You're right. Since Sarah's the only one with a key, if she and Melissa aren't back yet, we're stuck out here."

Nick had completely forgotten that his car had been their only mode of transportation, and with him now married to Jessica, that option was gone. He then thought about his uncle. "Maybe they got a ride from my uncle. We should still knock to see if he brought them back after the ceremony."

"Good point."

Walking up to the front door, she felt as if her life had become a whirlwind of events since she had returned to California. From stepping off the plane single, meeting Nick, seeing her aunt's dead body, Ms. Cecilia's murder, possibly becoming pregnant, marrying Nick, and now taking the first step in moving into his house, she honestly had no idea how she had managed to keep her sanity.

Knocking on the door, they were lucky, as Melissa answered it.

"What are you two newlyweds doing back here? Shouldn't you be at his house enjoying married life?"

"In our rush to become husband and wife, I forgot the step of packing my suitcase to bring it over to his house once the ceremony was over," Jessica answered, reading between the lines of her sister's subtlety.

"My apologies, Mrs. Powell. Come on in, then."

"Funny, Melissa."

"Well, you officially aren't a Parker anymore."

"But legally I still am."

"That's just a technicality."

"For now, yes." Jessica smiled at Nick.

Returning her expression, he followed her up to the guest bedroom. Waiting while she packed up her suitcase, he thought about succumbing to his desire of making love to her in the bed.

CHAPTER 30

"Do you remember what time Melissa said we needed to be at my aunt and uncle's house to leave for Kyle's uncle's yacht?" Jessica asked Nick as they lay in his bed together. Waking up to him was a regularity she had come to enjoy deeply.

"I think she said four fifteen. It's supposed to be really romantic at sunset." He enjoyed the feel of her bare skin against his, and he was happy he didn't have to leave her to head home and change clothes.

"Sounds enjoyable."

"Yeah, it does. But won't it be awkward for Sarah?"

"It turns out she might not end up coming after all. She still has many things to do for Aunt May's funeral service. She wants to get everything taken care of before she and Melissa return to New York City."

"Which means you'll get your double date after all."

"I will, and it may be the last one for a while."

"We'll still have another chance when I go with you."

She pulled him into a kiss for his reminder of that.

"What was that for?"

"I love that you take notice of what's important to me."

"I'll make sure to always do that, then," he teased.

"Honestly, Nick, I find it really endearing and it means a lot to me."

"Jessica, what's important to you is important to me. It's as simple as that."

"Are you trying to earn brownie points right now?"

"No, but how am I doing?"

Shaking her head at him, she said, "Good until you asked that question."

"Then isn't it a good thing I know how to seduce you into more?" He maneuvered her onto her back.

Looking up at him, she wrapped her arms around his neck. "I guess it's a good thing we've got the majority of the day for this."

"Yeah, it is."

Finally getting out of bed, Nick and Jessica got ready to go meet Melissa for their double date with her and Kyle.

Slipping on a pair of beige capris and a navy blue striped tank top with a dark blue left breast pocket and shoulder straps, Jessica finished her outfit with a pair of black flip-flops. Pulling her hair back into a quick ponytail, she was ready to go.

"I'm ready to go whenever you are." Jessica began unpacking her suitcase and putting her clothes in his closet while she waited for him.

"It won't take me long."

Grabbing a light blue T-shirt and jeans and adding a pair of dark blue and white boat shoes, he was dressed in a few minutes.

"Will we want to get a house with a walk-in closet for you?" He wondered how extensive her clothing collection was.

"A walk-in closet would be nice."

Coming up behind her and wrapping his arms around her, he said, "I can't wait until we're settled into our own home."

"Me too. Though we'll have to make sure there're at least two extra bedrooms."

"You're already thinking about a second baby—that is, if you're pregnant now."

"Yeah. But it's also just planning ahead."

"We can definitely do that." He gave her a kiss. "Or at least get a lot of practice in when we attempt a second one."

After kissing him back, she said, "We'd better go; otherwise, we're never going to leave your bedroom."

"You can always call your sister and tell her that we're still on our honeymoon."

"As nice as that sounds, no. Melissa would be too nervous to be alone on a yacht with a guy she just met. No, we need to go and provide her that reassurance."

"You're a good sister, you know that? Melissa and Sarah are lucky to have you." He released her from his arms.

"I feel the same with them. Now let's go before Melissa calls to ask me where we are."

Returning to being their chauffeur, Nick drove them to the dock. Once they arrived, Melissa called Kyle to come meet them.

With excitement, Melissa anxiously awaited the moment she would see him again. As each second passed, it dawned on her that she had never been this excited to see Cody. Sure, there was always at least some eagerness with him, but never anything like this.

CHAPTER 31

As Kyle neared the dock's entrance, he realized that from the time he'd said goodbye to Melissa at the club until now, he had already begun missing her.

When he finally locked eyes with her again, he could feel the spark from the other night. His immediate attraction to her was one thing, but when she smiled at him, it was as if his whole world was rocked to its core.

"Hi, Melissa. I'm glad I get to see you again." He gave her a respectful hug.

"Hi, Kyle ... and you too." She gave him that smile.

"I'm sorry Sarah couldn't come. I enjoyed getting to know her the other night."

"Yeah, me too. Unfortunately, there's still a lot that needs to get done for our aunt's funeral service, although she would've loved to see your uncle's yacht."

"Maybe another time, then." He guided the three down the dock and onto a large yacht with a table set for dinner. "I thought we'd eat while we watch the sunset." He showed them the romantic setup of fine china with red rose petals scattered around the center of the table.

"It smells delicious, Kyle. Thank you," Jessica complimented as Nick pulled out her seat for her.

Their entrée was lasagna with a side of vegetables covered in melted pimento cheese.

"Thanks. It was from an old family recipe." After pulling out Melissa's chair for her, Kyle sat down next to her.

With a choice of iced water or an expensive bottle of wine for their thirst, the four were set for their evening meal, as the dock's ambiance added the romantic view of the sunset.

However, as the conversation flowed easily among the four, Melissa began to wish that she and Kyle had opted for their own date. She knew that he was just trying to be respectful of her by not coming on too strong with the use of his uncle's yacht, but Melissa wanted to be alone with him.

She wanted to hold his hand and have a flirtatious conversation with him that could be turned into inside jokes later on in their relationship. Unfortunately, now it would be awkward to try to be romantic with him while her sister and brother-in-law were sitting across from them.

As she scooped up her last bite of lasagna, Melissa wondered if there was a way to let her sister know her desire—a way that wouldn't make it awkward for either Nick or Kyle. After all, if Kyle desired the same thing, then she was sure he would jump at the chance once something was suggested.

Briefly observing the closeness her sister and brother-in-law had kept with each other throughout the dinner, Melissa knew she had to come up with something. Glancing at their near-empty plates, she realized that they still had one course left: dessert.

"Now that your lasagna has pretty much been devoured, what's for dessert?" Melissa asked.

"Well, there's ice cream, I guess." He had spent so long making dinner that he'd completely forgotten about dessert.

"That sounds good. Why don't you show me our options?" Melissa urged.

"Would you two like some as well?" Kyle looked at Jessica and Nick as he got up from his chair.

Melissa shot Jessica a look that said, *Please say no.*

"No, thanks. Nick and I are pretty full from the lasagna. Thanks for the offer, though."

Smiling at Melissa's clear interest in Kyle, Jessica watched her slip her hand into his as they went down below.

"Melissa really likes Kyle, doesn't she?" Nick asked after seeing the interaction himself.

"Yep. I'm thinking she now wishes they were on this date alone."

"We could always leave and come up with an excuse later."

"No, we'll simply just stay up here while she has her time alone with him down there." Getting up from her seat, Jessica reached out her hand to him. "Come on—I want to go watch the sunset until the sky turns into a blanket of stars."

Taking her hand, Nick followed her to where they could lean against the yacht's railing while he held her in his arms.

Each couple was getting their own romantic ending to the date.

CHAPTER 32

Heading into the kitchen after finishing the last of the tasks for her aunt's funeral service, Sarah decided on leftovers for dinner. As she took out her options, she saw the box containing their aunt's will. Completely forgetting about it after getting the call about Ms. Cecilia not making it through surgery, she lifted off the lid and brought it over to the kitchen table. Creating her dinner from the leftovers, Sarah put it in the microwave to reheat before sitting down to read her aunt's last wishes.

Reading its contents, she was in complete shock. As she reached the last page of the document, she found a letter written to her and her sisters.

> *2/29/16*
>
> *Dear girls,*
>
> *If you are reading this, that means something has happened to me. I just want you three to know how much I love you. I greatly cherished the many years you girls came to visit your uncle and me. Those are priceless memories that I will never forget. Sadly, they had to end, but I promise you that I will never forget those years.*
>
> *By now, you will have read that I've left this house, all of its contents, and your uncle George's real estate investments to you. Be aware, though, that my maid,*

Ms. Cecilia, has become too nosy over the last few years of her employment. Despite her long withstanding service to me, she believes I owe her more than the wage we agreed upon years ago. It is because of this that I had to take the necessary precaution of hiding my will and this letter where I was sure no one would find it.

Sadly, I have since learned that she has secretly employed her husband, Damon, to uncover the whereabouts of it. Ms. Cecilia, her husband, and his uncle Gino now have their sights set on your uncle George's wealth. You three must not let her know anything about it when you find it; otherwise, the consequences might be deadly.

With all my love,
Aunt May

Damon Riley was Ms. Cecilia's husband? I've got to let Melissa and Jessica know! Sarah took out her phone to call Melissa. *The double date on his uncle's yacht must've been a trap!*

As Sarah scrolled through her phone to speed-dial her, she heard the front door open. "Hello? Who's there?"

It couldn't be Melissa; it was much too early for the foursome to have already ended their date night.

Seconds later, the microwave beeped to let her know her food was finished reheating, scaring her. Quietly opening the door to stop it before it beeped again, Sarah grabbed a knife before calling 911 instead.

Hearing the front door close, she immediately sunk down behind the island. *Maybe I can close the microwave door quietly and whoever's here won't know that I'm still in the kitchen.*

Her mind raced for an exit strategy. She had no idea who had broken in or if they had even heard the microwave beep. For all she knew, the intruder was walking around the house looking for something valuable to steal, with no intention of harming her.

As she hid behind the island in silence, she heard the 911 operator answer her call. Doing her best to stay as quiet as possible, she barely let out a whisper to the operator as she explained her situation.

With her heart racing, she prayed to God she would hear the front door close, letting her know it was safe again. But as the operator stayed on the phone, keeping her company and being a witness to the fear coursing through her body, Sarah heard the terrifying steps of the intruder make their way to the kitchen.

Tightening every muscle in her body, she tried to hide her phone just in case the intruder found her. As she was forced to play a game of hide-and-seek with the desperate hope of not being found, she heard the intruder's voice.

"They found the will!"

She could hear the papers being moved as the intruder went through them. Feeling her heart pound with each second that passed, she realized that the voice sounded familiar. Very familiar. *It's Damon, Ms. Cecilia's husband!*

Doing her damnedest not to give her hiding place away, she pushed down the desire to spring up from the floor and tell him that she knew everything. After all, she had no idea if he was carrying a weapon on him, and if he was, whether that weapon was meant to harm her.

Instead, she and the operator waited to see if he would take her aunt's will and leave. Closing her eyes, she now wished she had gone to see Kyle's uncle's yacht.

Waiting in desperation for him to finish looking at the will and leave, Sarah felt immobilized by her fear. Damon was here to uncover the secrets of her aunt's will. She just prayed to God that he also didn't uncover the secret of her hiding place.

With each page turn, Sarah could feel the loud thud of her heart beating. It was a miracle that the microwave had beeped when it had.

"Damn it! Where does it say it?" She heard him hurriedly search through the stack of papers. "It's got to be in here somewhere!"

Damon didn't know how long Nick and the sisters would be gone. But if they got back before he had found what he was looking for, he was prepared. He had made sure to bring a gun from his uncle's collection.

Paper after paper, he sifted through the information, hoping to hit the jackpot page. However, as he searched through legal jargon, a realization hit him. With his mindset solely on finding May Willard's will, he forgot to notice that the kitchen light was on. Not only that; someone had left Tupperware on the counter.

Pausing his page turning, he thought, *I wonder if that means one of the Parker sisters is still home?* With a devious smile on his face, he removed the safety from his uncle's gun. *This way, if something happens, I won't be to blame. Sorry, Uncle Gino.*

Sarah felt her heart catch. She wondered if he realized that she was still home—home and hiding.

"Hmm, I wonder which Parker sister is still home?" he said teasingly, unknowingly confirming Sarah's suspicion. "And if I interrupted their dinner?" He shifted his weight to move toward the microwave.

Remaining still, Sarah Parker readied the knife. If Damon was going to use his gun to kill her, she wasn't going to let it happen without a fight. Squeezing the knife's handle until her knuckles turned white, she was ready for him.

Peering over the island's countertop, Damon found Sarah Parker hiding with a knife tightly in her hand. "I've found you." His voice was haunting.

CHAPTER 33

"I know the truth, you son of a bitch!" Sarah sprang up, ready to fight.

"It doesn't matter now, does it?" He looked at her with a smirk. "I've got a gun, and you've got a kitchen knife. I wonder who's going to win this battle."

"That may be, but this kitchen knife won't stay clean by the end of it!"

Sarah knew her chances of survival were slim as he kept his gun pointed at her, but she was going to do her damnedest to defend herself.

"Should I let you take a jab at me just to give you a chance?" His eyes were pure evil as he relished in the taunting.

All Sarah could do was show him her defensive stance. As she looked back at him, the gun's safety off, she knew that the second she lunged at him, he would pull the trigger and that would be it. She just thanked God for having the opportunity to get one last moment with her sisters as they watched Jessica marry Nick. Having that as her last memory of her sisters caused a tear to fall.

"Don't tell me that the prospect of you about to be murdered by your aunt's murderer is making you cry." The maliciousness of his actions was heard through his voice.

With widened eyes at his confession, Sarah forgot about her weaker weapon and lunged her knife into him.

Feeling the horrendous pain as the sharp metal pierced through his shirt and into his skin, Damon was caught off guard.

He attempted to get one shot off, but Sarah was already on the offensive.

As more stabs met with more agonizing pain, he finally connected a bullet with Sarah's body. Watching her collapse where she had been hiding, Damon held his own wounded body. As blood coated his clothes and dripped onto the floor, he watched Sarah suffer from her own loss of blood.

"The bitch wasn't wrong." He glanced at the knife she had been clenching and saw his blood dripping from it.

But as his blood loss took its toll on him, he realized that he needed to hide before Melissa returned.

"I had a really nice time tonight, Kyle. Let me know when you get into New York City and I can give you that personal tour we talked about at the club." Melissa took her time in saying goodbye to him as Jessica and Nick waited for her in the car.

"I did too, and I definitely will." He smiled. "Is it okay if I give you a kiss?"

"Of course." She loved his chivalrous side.

Watching him cup her cheek with his right hand, she closed her eyes and felt his lips against hers. Magic. Pure magic.

"Your number is the first one I'll call the second I get into the city." He kept her close to him.

Smiling, she said a final goodbye to him before joining her sister and brother-in-law in his convertible.

As her brother-in-law drove them back to her and Jessica's aunt and uncle's house, Melissa couldn't help but wish she was already back in New York City, seeing her phone ring with Kyle's number on the caller ID. With a deep sigh, she decided that the second they got home, she was going to run upstairs to start packing.

Arriving back at their aunt and uncle's house, Melissa said goodbye to each before giving her sister a hug and heading inside.

But right as Nick was about to pull out of the driveway, he and Jessica heard her scream Sarah's name.

Turning off the engine, he and Jessica hurried inside to see what had happened.

"Melissa?" Jessica called out as Nick flung open the door.

"I'm in the kitchen." Her voice was shaky.

Rushing to her, they found Sarah lying on the kitchen floor. A bullet to her torso had caused a pool of blood to collect beside her. Lying loosely in her right blood-covered hand was the kitchen knife she had used to defend herself.

"Sarah!" Jessica screamed.

Hearing a voice come from Sarah's nearby cell phone snapped her out of it. "She called 911." But as Jessica reached for the phone to let the operator know what was going on, she heard a faint groan coming from her.

"She's still alive! Sarah's still alive!" Jessica continued as Nick took the phone from her to explain the situation to the operator.

As he listened to the operator, he instructed Jessica to get a dish towel and apply pressure to the wound until the paramedics got there. Following every instruction given to him, he relayed the information to Jessica to keep Sarah alive. Despite the significant amount of blood loss, he checked for a pulse. "Jessica's right. She's still alive, but just barely. Keep as much pressure on the wound as possible!" he directed her.

As Jessica remained kneeling on the floor, the towel completely soaked with her sister's blood, Damon appeared with his gun drawn. The operator, the only witness to their potential murders, remained on the phone.

"What the hell?" Nick exclaimed. He immediately saw the stab wounds Sarah had inflicted on him as she fought him for her life.

"You girls have just made this too easy for me. One bullet for each of you—and your aunt and uncle's fortune is mine!"

"Damon? You're Kyle's brother. What are you doing here?" Melissa was in shock.

Sarah tried to speak through her faint groaning, but her gunshot wound made each breath harder.

"The same thing I did to your aunt May." He prepared to release another bullet, but this time in Melissa's direction. Releasing the safety, he shifted his right index finger to the trigger.

Melissa's eyes went wide. She didn't know what to do. She wouldn't be able to escape the kitchen in time if he pulled the trigger, and she didn't have a weapon she could easily grab that would overpower his finger on the trigger. Her shocked body kept her frozen as her aunt's murderer stood ready to make her his next victim.

Nick felt helpless. Unless he could somehow knock the gun out of Damon's hand, his sister-in-law was about to be murdered right in front of him.

Despite the clear pain he was in from his own wounds, Damon remained in complete control over everyone. As he took in Melissa's terrified expression, he realized that with one single pull of his gun's trigger, he'd have only one more Parker sister to kill. Even with Jessica's attempt at trying to save her older sister's life, it was likely too late. Sarah had lost too much blood for the blood-drenched towel to make any difference. Smiling, he enjoyed the control.

"Or should I make you choose, Nick?" He realized the true power he now held. "Your sister-in-law or your wife first?" Damon glanced at Jessica, who maintained her desperate attempt to control Sarah's bleeding.

"You bastard!" He was in a nightmare! Regardless of whom he chose, both would die.

"On second thought, I'll have mercy on you." Damon pulled the trigger as the barrel stayed fixed on Melissa.

"No!" Nick screamed. He darted to protect Melissa.

Screaming bloody murder, Jessica silently prayed to God that Nick had been able to save her sister without taking the bullet himself.

With the bullet discharged, the room went silent. *What happened? Was Nick too late? Has Melissa been shot? Is Nick okay?*

So many questions ran through Jessica's mind as she remained on the floor with Sarah.

Then an even worse thought went through her mind. *Is Damon about to kill me next?* For all she knew, Damon could now be standing over her with his gun pointed at her, ready to end her life as well.

She was hesitant to look anywhere but at her sister. But as the realization that she might now be a widow entered her mind, she realized that she needed to take the chance. Right as she was about to, she heard Detective Murray's voice.

"Damon's down. It's all clear."

With her mind asking a thousand more questions, all she could get out was, "Over here! Sarah's been shot!"

Hearing the rustle of movement, she saw paramedics swarm into the kitchen with a gurney.

"Nick! Are Nick and Melissa okay?" Jessica swiftly got up as a paramedic traded places with her.

Detective Murray rushed to her side. "Are you okay, Jessica? Are you hurt anywhere?"

Watching Sarah be wheeled away to an awaiting ambulance, Jessica could barely focus her attention on answering his question. *How much blood has Sarah actually lost? God, please let her make it!*

"Jessica? Are you okay? Did Damon hurt you?"

"Damon? No, Damon didn't hurt me. How are Nick and Melissa?"

CHAPTER 34

With her system in shock, Melissa stayed behind Nick as he kept her guarded. He had made his body her barricade as the bullet came speeding toward her.

"Did you ... get shot ... instead?" Melissa asked him, her whole body still shaking.

"No. I think the bullet just grazed me." He could feel a slight burn on his arm. Looking at his skin, he could see the reddened area left behind.

"Thank you, Nick!" Her tears came flooding down when she realized what he had done for her.

"Of course. We're family now." Bringing her into his arms, he hugged her. "But now I need to know if Jessica's okay." He ended their embrace.

They got up, and Melissa watched him head over to her as she talked to Detective Murray.

"Jessica!" He came up beside her.

"Nick!" She collapsed into his arms, uncontrollably sobbing as he held her.

He could think of no words to say as he watched the police turn the Willards' kitchen into a crime scene.

"I'm just so glad you're okay!" Nick held her tightly to him.

He could see Damon's dead body waiting to be covered by the coroner. He couldn't believe it. Just a few hours ago, he and Jessica were on a yacht, enjoying a romantic evening together, and now Sarah was being rushed to the hospital, fighting for her life.

"Where's Melissa? Is she okay?" Jessica asked through tears.

"She's fine. I protected her." Nick looked back at her to see her talking to a police officer, no doubt giving him her statement.

Watching the aftermath of the horror that had just taken place, it was all Nick could do to console Jessica. With one sister now too close to the possibility of death and their aunt's murderer lying dead on the floor, he had no idea how the two of them were going to get through this.

Immobilized in his arms, Jessica replayed seeing Sarah, seemingly dead on the floor, and Melissa's attempted murder in her mind. Glancing over at Damon's lifeless body, she closed her eyes and imagined she was in a garden of her aunt's favorite flowers.

With the floral smell covering her anguish, she breathed a sigh of peace. Damon's desire for her aunt and uncle's wealth was not going to ruin her memories of their house or destroy the contentment she always felt with each visit.

"Nick, we need to go to the hospital," she whispered.

Nodding, Nick watched the coroner finally enter the kitchen. After pictures of the scene had been taken, Damon's body was carefully put into a body bag to be taken to the morgue. Nick's thoughts turned to the same process being used for the sisters' aunt. How fitting it was that their aunt's murderer was killed in her own house.

"Uncle John, am I good to take the girls to the hospital to see Sarah?"

"Yeah, Nick. Go right ahead."

With Damon now dead, Sarah's attempted murder was an open-and-shut case. Since the perpetrator had been killed, there wouldn't be a need for any witnesses to corroborate what had happened.

Driving the girls to the hospital to see if their sister had survived her gunshot wound was not how Nick had imagined spending his days as a newlywed.

Fortunately, with Damon no longer a threat to the sisters' lives, they could move on from this horrific night. They also now knew who had taken their aunt's life and the reason for it.

After arriving at the hospital, they were informed that Sarah was in surgery. However, her fight to live was far from over. With the bullet now out, she had lost so much blood that she needed a transfusion. What had taken seconds to cause was now taking hours to fix.

Jessica had never experienced so much tragedy in her life. It seemed like one thing after another. She could not wait for God to miraculously heal her sister and have life get back to normal.

Taking a seat in the waiting room, the hours slowly passed by and her shock from the night's events turned into tiredness. She thanked God that she had Nick and Melissa there for support.

Using Nick's right shoulder as her pillow, she closed her eyes as her body told her she'd had enough. It wasn't but a few minutes later when she felt him nudge her awake.

"Jessica. Jessica, wake up!"

Slowly opening her eyes, Jessica woke up to realize she was in Nick's bed. *Did I just dream it all? Is my aunt still alive?* She didn't know what was real and what was in her mind. *But I'm in Nick's bed, so that must mean that part was real.*

"Jessica, you need to get up or we're going to be late for our flight."

"Our flight?"

"Yes, our flight ... to pick up your mom from the psychiatric facility." Nick looked at her questioningly. "She's coming to live with us, or did you forget?"

"She is?"

"Jessica, are you okay?"

"I think so. Did Sarah survive?"

"Survive? Oh. You mean the gunshot?" Nick realized that she'd had the dream again. "Yes, she survived. She's now living in Florida with your dad and stepmom. Did you have the dream again?"

"Yeah. It's an endless nightmare."

"On the bright side, you get to relive our love story." He glanced down at her expanded belly. Their daughter's due date was nine months from their wedding date.

"While also reliving both of my sisters' attempted murders."

"So you take the bad with the good. At least your aunt's death brought me into your life and Kyle into Melissa's. You found out Sarah has strength in her that the three of you never knew she had—and you're both reconnecting with a parent."

"Speaking of, do you think it'll be weird moving into my aunt and uncle's house and making their room ours?

"No. Why should it? Their house is a two-story house big enough to fit our expanding family, and there's the extra help your mom will provide."

"True. I just hope Damon's death and my sisters' attempted murders won't make it hard to live there."

"Jess, if you start getting flashbacks whenever you're in the kitchen, we can always look for a new place—a place that will be our very own and where we can make our own memories with our kids and grandkids."

"That sounds perfect!" She got out of his bed and pulled him into a kiss.

As much as she would've loved getting to watch her daughter grow up in her aunt and uncle's house, without them there, it just wouldn't be the same.

To honor Sarah's strength and Aunt May's memory, she and Nick named their daughter after them. Sarah May Powell needed to have her own family memories, not ones borrowed from what had been her mother's favorite place on earth.

Printed in the United States
By Bookmasters